# *The* CORRUPTION *of* FATHER MIKE

## NORM O'BANYON

*Here's to fresh inspiration and entertainment!*

*Norm O'Banyon*

**outskirtspress**
DENVER, COLORADO

This is a work of fiction. The events and characters described herein are imaginary and are not intended to refer to specific places or living persons. The opinions expressed in this manuscript are solely the opinions of the author and do not represent the opinions or thoughts of the publisher. The author has represented and warranted full ownership and/or legal right to publish all the materials in this book.

The Corruption of Father Mike
All Rights Reserved.
Copyright © 2014 Norm O'Banyon
v3.0

Cover Photo © 2014 thinkstockphotos.com. All rights reserved - used with permission.

This book may not be reproduced, transmitted, or stored in whole or in part by any means, including graphic, electronic, or mechanical without the express written consent of the publisher except in the case of brief quotations embodied in critical articles and reviews.

Outskirts Press, Inc.
http://www.outskirtspress.com

ISBN: 978-1-4787-3723-0

Outskirts Press and the "OP" logo are trademarks belonging to Outskirts Press, Inc.

PRINTED IN THE UNITED STATES OF AMERICA

# Contents

U. S. Army ................................................................ 1
Discharged to a New life ........................................ 34
Student at the University of Portland ...................... 42
A New Path to Priesthood ....................................... 89
A Different Call ..................................................... 103
St Joseph's ............................................................. 115
Blessed Sacrament ................................................ 134
The Plot Thickens ................................................. 165
Reality Bites ......................................................... 176
Resignation and Realization .................................. 190
Paroled to New Possibilities .................................. 200
Concluding surprise .............................................. 207

The afternoons were his favorite, for sure. With band practice in fifth period he could pound on the drums, and then in sixth period he could pound on Brad Phillips in wrestling practice. Mike O'Malley wondered if he could ever qualify for any scholarships as long as Philips kept winning tournaments.

An irritating voice right behind him startled Mike. "Get your ass off my drums!" He turned around to find Ernie Carrel, the new sophomore, glaring at him.

"I said, 'Get off my drums, you jerk!'" The James Dean wanna-be, in his jeans and white T-shirt with rolled up sleeves, stepped toward Mike threateningly. "I'm going to kick your ass!"

Mike was still smiling when he said, "The only name I see on the drum is 'Ludwig', but if you think it's worth it, bring it on, Carrel." He remained seated at the drums, but set one foot firmly behind himself as a brace.

Amazingly, the smaller man lunged at him, swinging his fist. Mike shot an open palm at the chest of the advancing body, catching him by complete surprise. The powerful thrust drove the attacker back against the wall where he slid to a stop.

The metallic click of a switch blade opening was a sinister warning. Mike immediately got up to face the new challenge. "I said those are my drums, you big dummy." He advanced holding the knife low. "I'm going to cut you!" he growled as he swung.

Mike easily caught Carrel's wrist, neutralizing the threat, and using it as a lever as he pirouetted the attacker around into a choke hold. It took about ten seconds for Carrel to drop the knife, and Mr. Peterson, the Band Director who had witnessed the entire incident to run across the room. He led the limp attacker out of the band room to the vice principals office. Carrel was suspended from school for a week for the incident, and Mike forgot about it.

A couple hours later, as he was leaving school, however, he was reminded of it by Ernie Carrel standing in the middle of the sidewalk. As soon as Mike saw him, he stopped to assess the situation. A grinning Ernie spread his open hands to show there was no malice in the moment. "I'm sorry if I scared you," he said happily. "I asked around who the toughest senior might be."Your name and Phillips came up. Smiling weakly, he admitted, "He has already turned me down, so I had to come to you. I need your help, man."They were now standing close enough to talk quietly. "I have a problem," Ernie began. "There is a big wop that waits for me in the parking lot every afternoon. He says he's going to key my car if I don't pay him ten bucks." He shook his head in angry frustration. "Cripes, he's bleeding me dry!"

"And how is this my business?" Mike asked.

"Well, if you will walk out to my car with me, and convince the fat shit to leave me alone, I will pay you the ten bucks."

With a smile that matched Ernie's, Mike said, "Since you put it that way, let's get to it."

The confrontation didn't take long once they walked up to Ernie's '46 Ford. Mike asked the big fellow leaning against the car, casually turning an ice pick in his hand, "Is this your wheels?" He pointed to the '41 Chevy parked next to Ernie's.

"Mind your own business or you might get…"

The words were cut off as Mike snatched the ice pick out of his hand. Stepping over to the Chevy, he drove the sharp point of the pick into a white sidewall tire. "The next time I do this it will be in your neck, wop." He jerked the ice pick out and threw it over the chain link fence onto the railroad tracks. "You might get to a filling station before that goes completely flat." The would-be extortionist jumped into his car and left with a squeal of burning rubber.

Ernie burst out with a giggle, saying, "Holy shit, how did you do that? It was like he was frozen, and you snapped that right out of his hand! That was amazing!"

Now that it was over, Mike could grin a bit. "Naw, it has to do with reaction time. We all have at least a half second before we can react to a threat. For the determined, that is enough time to gain an advantage. I'll show you; do you have a quarter?"

When Ernie nodded, Mike said, "Show it to me." Ernie reached in his pocket, drew out his hand, and as he was opening it, Mike's hand flashed in to grab the coin. "Hey, I wasn't ready," he protested.

"Neither was Tubby. Now I will trade you this quarter for the ten you owe me." The unlikely friendship of Mike and Ernie was created.

Through the winter and spring they were frequently seen in the hallways together. Ernie knew Mike's schedule of classes, and was usually waiting in the hall for his large friend. They didn't talk a whole lot, but Ernie's grin just from being in the shadow of his protector, was reward enough. He seemed to have plenty of money and girl friends that he offered to share with Mike. But always the answer was that the big guy was busy with wrestling, hoping for that illusive scholarship.

Just before Easter, Ernie caught up with Mike as he was leaving school. "Hey Big Guy, you work at Caesar's Furniture don't you?" When Mike grunted an affirmative answer, Ernie caught his arm and said, "It would be a good idea if you catch a sudden case of the flu. Don't go to work this afternoon. I've heard there is going to be some trouble there."

At first Mike wanted to argue with his diminutive friend; but when Ernie said, "I'm serious. Guys from Levine's are threatening to visit tonight. You might wreck your chances for a scholarship." The matter was settled. Mike didn't have much to do at the furniture warehouse anyway. Nobody would miss him.

The next morning's news reported a gang fight at Caesar's Furniture Warehouse, that had eventuated in police arrests and the fire department had to put out a fire that could have been damaging. Mike wondered how Ernie had come into the information to warn him. Thank goodness he had!

# U. S. Army

By the end of April, Mike had to admit that there would not be a college wrestling team interested in him, and Ernie had been sent to Juvenile Detention for breaking into a gun shop. Before the Woodrow Wilson High School class of 1951 graduated, the Vice Principal had counseled Mike that the U.S. Army would be a place in which he could both serve his country in the Korean Conflict, and take advantage of the GI Bill to help him with future college expenses. On one of his infrequent weekends at home, Mike's dad, a long-haul truck driver, had agreed with the advice. His mom, a weary waitress had said it was the best they could do. His wrestling coach had encouraged him to listen, and do exactly as he was instructed. He would do fine.

Fort Benning, located in Georgia, was hot by any comparison to Portland, but in July it was stifling. The three days on the train had provided enough time to meet some of the other recruits, and realize that they were all overwhelmed with this change in their lives. The first four days in the sprawling base was the most humiliating. It seemed to Mike that every human dignity was being denied them, but he remembered his coach's advice, and tried his best to comply with every order. By the second week he was no longer afraid he would lose his mind. He listened well and learned.

By the fourth week he had qualified as basic marksman both with a pistol and a rifle. He was most outstanding, however, in hand-to-hand combat. With his wrestling experience and knowledge of Judo, he was at least as good as his instructors, although he wanted to keep that a secret. There was no sense in antagonizing anyone else. When paired with another recruit, he was careful not to hurt them or beat them by very much.

When the ten-week training was over, the shots for every known disease administered, and indoctrination as complete as thick skulls would allow, Private O'Malley was assigned to four more weeks of specialized training in Military Police preparation. To his surprise the training revealed that his weapon of choice was not the .45 side arm he had scored high on, but a pair of night sticks. With a baton in each hand he could defeat multiple adversaries. He and eleven other PFCs were finally flown on a cargo plane to Yokosuka Japan, where their duties included the protection and over-sight of G.I.s who were on R and R from Korea. It was an easy assignment, if somewhat disgusting. Mike found himself making allowances for the behavior of battle-weary soldiers as long as they were not hurting themselves or others. A fall and winter, not unlike those wet ones he had experienced in Portland, slowly took their place on the calendar.

A New Year's brawl set his reputation for crowd control. A group of local Japanese tough guys, perhaps still smarting from the loss of the war, moved into the USO, intent on creating havoc. They had coordinated their trouble-making to start at the edge of the dance floor and push in toward the middle. There they intended to deliver a severe beating to the soldiers who might be slightly inebriated to begin with.

Fortunately, Mike's MP Patrol Jeep was less than a block away when the fight started. The fleeing partiers were a call for help. When Mike entered the hall, he had a baton in each hand, secured with lanyards. It was easy for him to identify the Japanese assailants, which he began methodically eliminating from the contest. There was plenty of screaming and swearing. But the most notable sound was the crack of the nightsticks and the thud of victims on the floor. He overwhelmed at least seven before he was targeted by the remaining troublemakers. They formed a semicircle in front of him and charged. The story that has lingered longest is that he got half of them before they could get close enough to throw a punch or kick. Then he caught the leader of the pack on the point of his shoulder and sent the man in a moaning crumple on the floor. The fight was over. Those who could run, did. The Japanese police finally arrived to remove the ones who couldn't. The Commandant's office received a communication from the chief of police, praising the deft skill of the MP who could have crippled or killed the trouble-makers, "but showed restraint and skill by keeping his blows to the shoulders, elbows and knees. In the history of the Japanese, those so trained were called 'Samaria', and honored with great respect. We do not know the name of this warrior, but we hope that you do, and will give him our deep appreciation for his skill and mercy."

The cherry trees were finishing their spectacular bloom when Mike heard the announcement of a new assignment. "Hey O'Malley," the Master Sergeant called. "You must have done O.K. with the BAR in boot camp. They want you to report to 79th Ordinance for reassignment. It looks like you are going to Korea." They were words that Mike had dreaded, but fully expected. He would recall forever the date, 3 July, 1952; it was his nineteenth birthday!

The crowded DC3 carried them to the airfield at Ch'orwan, Korea, where they threw their gear onto an open truck and piled in on top of it. In the distance they could hear the heavy thumping of bombs detonating. It was a bumpy and ominously forewarning ride to the staging area.

The young Sergeant that greeted them led them to a fairly large tent with a couple dozen cots. Mike wondered if they might be the same age. "This will be your last clean sleep for a while." The Sergeant gave weary directions. "Take advantage of it. There is a chow tent up the road about two hundred yards. You are responsible for your own tray and utensils. Lose them and you don't eat." His crooked smile showed no humor.

"So, I'm supposed to give you a history lesson as to why we are here," the young man began a speech that sounded under-written and over-used. "To some of us it is still a mystery. Let me say that it started at the surrender of the Japs in '45. Japan had held Korea since the early part of the century; with their surrender, the Allied Forces had to do something with it. It's a little like Berlin; Russia got the east half and the Allies got the west. Here, the 38th parallel was the dividing line. Russia got the north half of Korea, and we got the other."

"Politics will screw it up every time, won't it? June 25th of '50, a Battalion of North Korean Communists crossed the 38th and started kicking ass. They were sent home by UN Peacekeepers; that means 90% were U.S. Army and a few South Koreans. Then the Chinese People's Liberation Army (PLA) joined with the People's Republic of China Army (PRC) funded and supplied by Russia, to come at us like waves in the oceans. For two years we have killed them until they can't climb over the dead bodies. Then there will be a pause, and a few days later they will come again, usually at night. Imagine if you can, Americans fighting Chinese for the right of the Korean people to have a democratic half of their old country."

"A month ago there was a hell of a fight for outpost 10 on hill 255. You might have heard the news from Porkchop Hill. Two platoons of infantry from the 181st took just about an hour to clear two companies of chinks from the hill. But the next outpost east is Number 11 on hill 266. It's a different story. We fight to clear it, and they send in artillery big time. We ease off and they recapture the outpost. We send in artillery and air strikes, and they ease off and we retake it. That samba has been going on for a month, while the peace talks are continuing. I think we are keeping the hostilities going to remind them that there is a war going on out here. They are just now bombing the shit out of it. Maybe you could hear the detonations."

"In a couple days you will become part of the fresh meat to take 266, which the Brass is calling 'Old Baldy,' probably because it has been so blasted not even rocks can grow up there. You'll be added to Company A of the 180th Infantry Division." Not waiting for any questions, if some had not understood his information, he asked, "Who is Peters?" When a hand was cautiously raised, the Sergeant said, "You will be in charge of the flame thrower, and Martinson?" He looked around until another hand indicated the chosen one. "You will pack his flammable. Who is the patty, O'Malley?" Mike raised his hand. "You've drawn the big straw, the Browning. You'll also have an eighteen pound field pack of ammo. Don't burn it up all at once. The rest of you will have M1s, which you will check out today, and field strip and clean. Do you understand all of this?" He didn't expect any response, other than nodding heads and furrowed brows, which he got. "Chow is at 1600 hours. Be ready." He walked out without another word.

Mike selected an available cot to hold his duffle bag. He glanced at his watch determining there was enough time for him to get to the armory and back by supper time. Several of the others were busy writing letters and for just a moment he pondered who might want to hear from him. For just another second he wondered what Ernie might be up to; had he received a sentence for his burglary? He set off to find that Browning Automatic.

The Corporal checked the list to find his name. "Yup, there you are. How did you manage to draw the winning ticket for this bad girl? She'll dance your feet off."

As the rifle was being unwrapped, Mike snorted, "Just luck and good looks I guess. Say can I have that canvas cover? I'll bring it back, but it might keep the action a bit cleaner."

"I like your attitude, brother," the corporal said with a warm smile. "Most of the guys that come in here are so scared they can't think about anything except their next bowel movement, and you are promising to return a canvas sack. I like that a lot! What's your name?"

"I'm Mike O'Malley, from Portland Oregon. Maybe you could look me up when this is over, and we'll share a beer." He enjoyed an inward smile, talking like a tough guy when he was too young to buy beer.

"Yeah, I really like your attitude. Are there many O'Malley's in the phone book?" They joked together for another minute or two, but Mike knew he had work to do cleaning the rifle.

He was near the front of the line at 16:00, wondering if he could put enough food on his tray to fill the hollow ache in his stomach. On second thought, the ache was probably more out of dread than hunger, as he heard another round of heavy concussions from the top of the hill. A sign on the flap of the mess hall announced that the Chaplain would be available for a chapel service here at 19:00. Captain C.C. Blake was widely known as the "flying chaplain." Mike thought, "What the hell? I've never been in a church, and I haven't anything better to do." He had no way of knowing how completely true that was.

By 19:00 there were only a few stragglers standing around the mess hall. The huge tent was empty except for the chaplain and a table with a candle, cross, and trays of some sort. After peering in, Mike decided to wait until a half dozen others had gone in, before he eased in and took a seat near the back. A few more entered until there might have been three dozen. Finally, an officer stepped to the front.

"Good evening gentlemen. My name is Charlie Blake." His sleeves were rolled up a bit, and he had a green scarf around his neck, but his Captain's bars were easy to identify. "I'm really glad we can spend a few minutes together. These are difficult days, and I know you have things to do." He was handing out some printed cards. "I like the words of Teresa of Avila, a sixteenth century nun, who said, 'From silly devotions and sour-faced saints, good Lord, deliver us.'" Mike liked him immediately. As the chaplain finished handing out the cards, he said, "Tuck these in your pocket when we're done here. It might be easy reading in the days ahead."

"When the church was in its infancy, the people worshiped by sharing their thoughts together. Some times that worked, but most of the time it didn't, so little by little they collected words that had power to focus and encourage them. The card I just distributed is one of those collections. It's called the *Te Deum*, which is Latin for the first words of the prayer: 'You are God.' Let's read it together, or just listen if you'd rather."

"You are God and we praise you; you are the Lord, and we acclaim you; You are the Eternal Father; all creation worships you. To you all angels, all the powers of heaven, Cherubim and Seraphim sing in endless praise, Holy, Holy, Holy Lord, God of power and might; Heaven and earth are full of your glory. The glorious company of apostles praise you; the noble fellowship of prophets praise you; the white-robed army of martyrs praise you; throughout the whole world the holy Church acclaims you, Father of Majesty unbounded; you are the true and only Son worthy of all worship, and the Holy Spirit advocate and guide." Most of the words were strange to Mike, but reading them with the others was causing him to feel light and warm. "You Christ are the King of glory, the eternal Son of the Father. When you became man to set us free you did not abhor the virgin's womb. You overcame the sting of death and opened the Kingdom of Heaven to all believers. You are seated at God's right hand in glory. We believe that you will come to be our judge. Come then Lord and help your people, bought with the price of your own blood; and bring us with your saints to glory everlasting."

"And when Jesus taught his disciples to pray together," the chaplain smiled warmly at the bowed heads, "he gave them these words: 'Our Father in heaven, hallowed be your name, your kingdom come, your will be done on earth as it is in heaven. Give us today our daily bread. Forgive us our debts, as we forgive our debtors. And lead us not into temptation, but deliver us from the evil one." A smattering of voices concluded, "For thine is the kingdom, the power and the glory forever. Amen"

"Now let me read for you a selection from St. Matthew's Gospel, because I'll bet there is no Gideon Bible in your hotel room." A chuckle was shared by most of the men. "Listen to one of the greatest stories told in scripture: Matthew 7:24-27. At the conclusion of the Sermon on the Mount Jesus said", the Chaplain began to read from a well worn Bible, "Everyone then who hears these words of mine and does them, will be like a wise man who built his house upon the rock; and the rain fell, and the floods came, and the winds blew and beat upon that house, but it did not fall, because it had been founded on the rock. Everyone who hears these words of mine and does not do them will be like a foolish man who built his house upon the sand; and the rain fell, and the floods came, and the winds blew and beat against that house, and it fell, and great was the fall of it."

The Chaplain looked at his listeners, as though sharing a secret, "Every listener who heard Jesus speak those words immediately knew three inescapable facts about the future." Chaplain Blake took a large breath.

"Every listener knew that the story contained a warning about an approaching storm. It is coming for everyone, the good and the not so, the faithful and the less than. There is no immunity to the storm; it came to the wise as well as the foolish. There is in fact a testing which will reveal the hidden strengths and weaknesses of every life. That was the first thing the listeners knew."

"But they also knew there was an inspiring word of hope. The course of events had still not been finally settled. There is a thrilling announcement contained in just five words in the heart of the story. It was this: 'But it did not fall!' 'But it did not fall!' Yes the rain fell; but the house did not fall. The floods came and beat against it – but it did not fall! The winds blew and pounded against it, but the house did not fall! Isn't that wonderful? God wants your life to have that sort of a conclusion! Yes, the storm raged against him; he was outnumbered and under equipped, but the house did not fall! We are free to choose the conclusion to the story. Friends, no decision that we ever make is more decisive or important than this: upon what are we going to build the house?"

As Mike listened he understood that the Chaplain was not speaking only about the story, but about his present and future action. "What am I going to be able to build? And on what?" Mike wondered.

"Thirdly," the Chaplain continued, "those listeners knew that action was required of them. Jesus had said, 'anyone who hears these words of mine *and does them,*' there's the clue. At the risk of oversimplification, I will point out three things Jesus wants us to hear and do."

"The first is the very heart of the Sermon on the Mount. Jesus says, 'Therefore do not be anxious, saying, what shall we eat? Or what shall we drink? Or what shall we wear? For the Gentiles seek all these things, and your heavenly Father knows that you need them all. But seek ye first his kingdom and his righteousness and all these things will be yours as well

Therefore do not be anxious about tomorrow, for tomorrow will be anxious for itself, but let the day's own troubles be sufficient for the day.' Now I want you to know that I am sitting right next to you listening to this word, because we have lots to be anxious about don't we? Right on the other side of this mountain there is an army looking to destroy us. I'm more than a little anxious about that. But I am more aware of a powerful God who offers us a confidence that is beyond description, a peace that can't be measured, and an eternal kingdom that is more powerful. Can you focus on that? Can you feel the anxiety releasing its grip and going away? Henry Ford once said, 'Whether you think you can, or think you can't, you're right!'"

"The second thing this story points out that Jesus wants us to hear and do, is to give freely. If you think he is talking about passing the plate, there are greater treasures we can give. We are to give forgiveness; didn't we just pray that we want God to forgive our debts, as we forgive our debtors? We can give freely of encouragement, or admiration, even understanding; we can applaud the grunt next to us who holds up his end and doesn't blink. If you can give those kindnesses you will discover that they are of far more value than whatever might be dropped in an offering plate, for if you can do that, you will know the third thing Jesus asks us to hear and do."

"You remember the tremendous affirmation Jesus gave his followers: 'You are the light of the world. A city set upon a hill cannot be hidden, nor do men light a lamp and put it under a bushel, but on a stand, and it gives light to all the house. Let your light shine before men, that they may see your good works and give glory to your Father who is in heaven.' The third word is clear: let it shine. When the light of Christ shines through you, something wonderful happens, not only in your life but in those around you."

"The people of St. Augustine Florida, which is the oldest occupied town site in our country, put up a huge cross, made of steel and stone. Yes they have terrible storms, even tornadoes and hurricanes, but always in the midst of the storm they can point to the cross, and know that they can make it through. It did not fall! Do you get that? It did not fall! It reminds me of the old gospel song: 'My hope is built on nothing less than Jesus' blood and righteousness. I dare not trust the sweetest frame, but wholly lean on Jesus' name. On Christ the solid rock I stand, all other ground is sinking sand, all other ground is sinking sand.'"

"When the storm pounds on you, remember this verse, 'But it did not fall, because it had been founded on the rock!'"

Mike realized that he had been listening to nothing other than the chaplain. He wasn't aware of the distant battle noise, nor the conversations of men outside. He wasn't sure that he could remember it all, but he would try.

Once again the chaplain held up the cards that had been handed out saying, "Turn the card over for a prayer we can say together. It's the Coventry Cathedral Prayer." He waited until he was sure everyone had theirs. "Pray with me: 'Father forgive the hatred which divides nation from nation, race from race, class from class, Father forgive. The covetous desires of men and nations to possess what is not their own, Father forgive. The greed which exploits the labors of men and lays waste the earth, Father forgive. Our envy of the welfare and happiness of others, Father forgive. Our indifference to the plight of the homeless and the refugee, Father forgive. The lust which uses for ignoble ends the bodies of men and women, Father forgive. The pride which leads to trust in ourselves and not in God, Father forgive. Amen."

The chaplain explained the final part of the service, the serving of the sacrament of Holy Communion. He made it clear that all were welcome to take the bread and cup. He said another prayer and once again invited all to come. The men stood to form a line before him but a few left, apparently choosing to end the service. A plate with small chunks of bread was offered, and a tray with small cups of juice followed. Mike listened to the chaplain's voice.

"Ask and it will be given you, seek and you will find, knock and it will be opened." The line moved slowly. "Be assured of this: God loves you; God forgives you; God has a plan for you; and even now equips you with faith." The line was shorter. "Those who hope in the Lord will renew their strength; they will soar on wings like eagles; they will run and not grow weary, they will walk and not be faint." Mike took a portion of bread, and then the cup. Suddenly he felt that whatever tomorrow might bring, it would be alright, maybe difficult, but manageable. As he walked out of the mess hall he felt a calmness like never before. He pondered it as he walked back to his own tent, aware of a weariness, and yet an excitement.

"Hey, O'Malley," he was greeted as he stretched out on his cot, "I didn't know you were religious." It was probably said as a slur, but nothing could dull the quiet peace he felt.

"I guess I am now," he answered with a new confidence.

The tent was still dark when the young Sergeant returned for reveille. "Wakey, wakey, wakey, ladies." His irritating voice and manner was not the way to climb out of a good sleep. "Grab your sox's and hit the deck, we have serious business today." The sleepy heads were rising from warm pillows. "We're going to eat early this morning at 0700. By 0800 you must have your duffle packed and be ready for a field inspection. Keep your mess kit in your field bag; it will be the only thing aside from your rifle and ammo that you will need for the next three days. Leave everything else here." Once again he simply turned and walked out.

Minutes later, standing in the chow line, Mike thought he was nervous enough to be sick. He had that bitter taste in his dry mouth like before a wrestling match. Then he remembered the card in his pocket. He read the *Te Deum* slowly, then again. It did help! He was more calm. What was that quote from Henry Ford? "Whether you think you can, or think you can't.... you're right!"

At the inspection, Mike stood at parade rest beside his cot. His blanket was properly folded, his duffle closed and clearly tagged with his name; his ammo pack looked out of place with his mess kit on it, and the Browning rested in the opened canvas cover. He was sure that he had listened, and complied to the command. Several were cited for additional material. When the Sergeant approached, Mike snapped to attention.

It only took a glance to see that he had prepared by the book. "It takes an Irishman to get it right?" the Sergeant quipped. "But what the hell is the canvas bag about?" He was about to jerk it out from under the Browning.

"It's to keep it clean, Sergeant," Mike said loudly. "We were told it would be pretty dirty up there. I don't want to jam the auto feature." Then a bit more playful, he added, "I promised the Corporal I'd bring it back clean." There were a couple who snickered and received a glare from the Sergeant, but finally he allowed a bit of a grin to ease the moment. "You mustn't break a promise," he said as he stepped to the next cot. Outside the sound of diesel trucks could be heard queuing up.

"Two tents to a truck," the course instructions were shouted. "Pack in tight." Mike began to shuffle toward the truck nearest their tent. With an eighteen pound ammo pack and a sixteen pound rifle, he didn't want any more weight to wrestle. The first of thirty trucks was beginning to lumber up the hill. In all, 1,370 men were on the move. At about 35 miles per hour it took them only an hour and a half to reach the embarkation point. From there it was a three mile hump on foot.

The top of Old Baldy was a jigsaw of barbed wire, mines and trenches. Since the Chinese had shelled and strafed the top all day yesterday, they assumed it was their turn to occupy hill 266. HQ had, however, ordered both the 180th Infantry and 171st Field artillery to move into an attack position. This might give the peace talks folks something to chew on.

It was still before noon when Mike saw the Sergeant making his way through the crowded trench. When he spotted Mike, he waved urgently for him to move forward. "First Lieutenant Blount is looking for a long gun. I'm glad I found you." It was apparent he had the same before-match jitters as everyone else. But he also had enough humor to ask, "Is it still clean?" They made their way through the twists and turns of the trench until they finally approached the main stem. "Keep your head down here. We are within easy pot-shot distance from the slopes." Mike had not heard that term.

A 1st Lieutenant came up and speaking with a southern

drawl, said, "Good to see you son. We've lost four good boys to that sombitch out there." He pointed into the area of wire and mines. "It took me a time to find the little bugger. Do you see that radio antenna?" He was looking through binoculars and pointing at a tower about six hundred yards away. "Now looky up yonder at what looks like a bag of rags on it, do you see it?" Mike was squinting to try to make out anything like a target. Then a sudden reflection caught his eye. In the dirt just above their heads, a bullet sent shards splattering.

"Damn him to hell," the Lt. growled. "Put that ought-six on him and knock him off the perch. Can you do that for me?" Mike was taking the canvas sleeve off the Browning, thinking , "If you think you can…" He popped a magazine in the rifle and jacked a shell in the chamber. He switched it to "auto," and peered down the long barrel to the open iron sights, calculating at that range he would need to hold at least a foot high, maybe a tiny bit more. He saw another flash and shouted, "Down." The bullet hit just above his head .

"Come on, son, send something his way," the Lt. moaned.

Thwack, thwack, thwack, the Browning barked.

"God damn it, you missed him," the Lt. groaned. "Hit him agi…" Then with a jubilant voice he said, "Hold on here, son. His rifle just fell. His leg is sliding off the platform. He must be tethered on. Oh Jesus, he is hanging there deader than a turd. Great shot, son! That was better than a 300 yard 3 wood! What is your name?" He had a smile as wide as a golfer who just broke par.

"O'Malley, sir, Mike O'Malley." He was feeling a numbness; he had just killed a man.

Turning to the Sergeant, the Lt. said, "Sergeant White will

you put that man's name in the book for me?" Looking at Mike again, he asked, "Since we have such a good thing going here, would you be up for another exercise?"

Mike was feeling the rush of adrenaline, and knew that it could get him in trouble. "I'm just a grunt, so I always say 'yes,' like a cheap date on Saturday night." His wide smile hid the fact that he was scared to death, and hardly aware of his senses.

"Son," the Lt. almost laughed out loud, "this is war, and we are not supposed to be having this much fun." Obviously he was feeling the effects of adrenaline as well. "I wonder," he directed his question to the Sergeant, "if you two could shimmy out the end of the trench here so you could, using that Browning, clear that cross trench that is occupied by slopes. Then you can use the radio, Sergeant, to contact the Field Artillery base with these coordinates to blast the hell out of their position with frags. Stay in contact, so you can adjust the fire and keep it away from us as much as possible. You know, one of those little pussycats could spoil your whole day."

Mike knew about shinnying up a tree, but he had no idea what shimmy was all about, and finally decided it just meant 'sneak.'

They went back along the trench about a hundred yards before they found a small depression they could use for cover as they crawled out in the open. Briefly Mike wondered if there might be mines in this area, then as quickly tried unsuccessfully to forget it. Along their way, the Sergeant would ease his head up to check on their progress, as they closed on the cross trench. "Another few yards should put us in a perfect firing position. Give me the ammo pack and I'll feed the magazines to you." He had thought through a very workable action.

Mike spread the bipod supports for the gun, and when the Sergeant nodded, he eased his shoulder into the rifle butt. His targets were less than fifty yards away when he began to fire. Thwack, thwack, thwack. Three rounds a second took only eight seconds to empty the first magazine. Men were tumbling in the trench before him like pins at a bowling alley. There was no place they could hide. With a smooth reload, Thwack, thwack, thwack; Bullets were biting into the dirt around them, but as the Browning was working its way up the length of the trench, there was no accuracy in the defensive fire. Thwack, thwack, thwack. Another magazine, and then another, he was targeting men now over two hundred yards away. The artillery must have been ready to fire for Mike could hear the whine of incoming shells. They were set with proximity fuses, designed to explode about a hundred feet off the ground, sweeping the area below them in shrapnel. The Sergeant tapped Mike on the shoulder to cease fire. Their work was finished. The artillery shells fell for another four minutes, as they hugged the ground. Then the top of Old Baldy was still as a morgue. Mike counted eleven empty magazines; he had fired over 300 rounds. His shoulder throbbed in pain; he was sure there would be a big bruise.

They crawled back to the trench the way they had come, not sure if there could still be enemy fire. There was none! The tally of the battle casualties was estimated at 2,700 Chinese dead, more than two Divisions; and two American dead, with two more wounded.

Lt. Blount was like a little boy in his delight. "Well done, Sergeant White! You were heroic!' Turning to Mike he continued to praise, "And you, Corporal O'Malley, will be heralded as one of the battle giants! Great job to both of you!" The barrel of the Browning was still too hot to touch.

When Mike looked at the Sergeant and mouthed "Corporal?" he just nodded and said, "You earned it in spades. I thought I was along to take over when you froze, but you were a machine, an animal." His smile was huge. "I'm proud to be with such a warrior." He stretched out his hand to shake Mike's.

By mid-afternoon the news was passed around that trucks were on their way to pick up the 180th personnel; the 171st would establish secure boundaries for outpost 11. The lucky ones would have a hot supper in the mess tent, while the others would dine on K rations. Before gratefully pulling the blanket over himself for the night, Mike was diligent to clean and oil the Browning, treating it like the good soldier it had been.

In the morning while he was in the chow line, Mike watched two of the new F-86 jet fighters whiz overhead. Suddenly he felt his chin quiver, and he had to swallow hard to keep down a sob. "What the hell?" he asked silently "What's this all about?" But he had a barely controllable urge to cry! A big breakfast didn't help, but he thought a nap might. All day long he felt like picking a fight with anyone, and resented the feeling as pure foolishness. His world seemed to be coming apart. He managed to get through the day without hurting someone, but only by reading his card, several times.

The next day at lunch, those dark feelings were still nagging him. When Mike saw the announcement that there would be a chapel service at 1900 he felt a wave of relief. All through the day he counted the hours. When it was finally time, Mike didn't stall around while others entered. He found his place in the back and held his breath. About half as many seats were taken as Mike remembered from the last time. Maybe what he had was a contagious bug going around. There was a gnawing fear that this sad feeling was not something that he could get over, that would just go away. Finally the chaplain began.

"Good evening, gentlemen, I'm Charlie Blake, your mobile Chaplain, one of three here in South Korea." As he was handing out a card, he said, "I understand it has been a rough week for you all. Shall we begin with prayer?" When the heads immediately bowed, he said softly, "Gracious God of bright mountaintops and dark valleys, grant unto us as we come to you, gratitude for all your gifts; sorrow for our sins, trust in your power and will to aid us. So grant that in these brief moments together we might find forgiveness for the past; strength for the present; confidence that the future can bring nothing that in your strength we cannot handle, through Christ Jesus our Lord. Amen."

When Mike looked up, he was surprised that Sergeant White was sitting next to him. When the chaplain invited them to read the *Te Deum* together, Mike smiled as the Sergeant pulled a very rumpled card from his shirt pocket. Obviously he had used it even more than Mike had used his. They read together, words that were becoming familiar, even if they were not fully understood. Then they prayed the Lord's Prayer, and Mike felt that his world was coming back together.

"Before I open the Gospel of Luke for us, I'd like to share a little bit of Bible background so you can better understand the emotional impact of the reading. In my imagination I see a boy from a prominent Roman family who loves watching the parades of men in breastplates, with swords and shields, wearing helmets with colored plumes. He dreams of being one of these proud men. One day he enlists, and begins the arduous task of discipline and duty. He works hard and is a good soldier. He's promoted; eventually, he becomes what he has dreamed of being – a centurion. They were tough and strong. They were the commanding officer of the basic fighting unit called a Century – one hundred men. There were ten centurions in a cohort, and sixty centurions in a legion. Does that sound like a Company, Battalion, and Regiment? Perhaps this Centurion had seen many battles; perhaps he had seen the terror of war and had sickened of the brutality. We know that a few years before this incident reported by Luke, there was an uprising of the Jews near Sepphoris, a town just a few miles from Nazareth. The Jews hated the foreign oppression and the occupying army. They tried to overthrow the Roman yoke. It was decided to make an example of their actions. A Roman legion came in and crucified two thousand Jews! Crosses lined the roadside between Sepphoris and Nazareth. It was a shocking, terrible sight. As far as the eye could see there were Jews on crosses writhing in pain as they died." Suddenly Mike remembered what the trench on the top of the hill looked like as he fired into the melee of hundreds of men. "Jewish people never forgot that moment," the chaplain continued. "I'm sure that it made a deep impression on the Roman soldiers as well – perhaps even upon this centurion. Perhaps something happened in the heart of this soldier. As you will see from the text, an amazing relationship existed between this soldier in the army of the occupation, and a defeated people."

"Try to imagine the plight of the Jewish nation – hardly thirty miles wide and a hundred and twenty miles long – a country with no army, no real wealth, but with a long stubborn dream of freedom and liberty. Furthermore, imagine living in a country that had been occupied by a long list of bullies – the Babylonians, the Assyrians, the Persians, the Greeks, the Parthians, and for the last forty years the most powerful empire in the ancient world, the Romans had overwhelmed them. Imagine that the most important thing in your life was the worship of God and the keeping of his law. You should know that the Romans worshipped idols and most recently, Pilot, the Roman Governor, had placed the image of an eagle over the entrance of the temple itself, and to top it off, the Emperor called himself the son of god. Now that we know something about the sense of raw power against the depth of hurt, and the patriotism of the people who heard these words for the first time, we can open our lives and visualize the action in Luke 7:1-9." The chaplain finally opened his well worn Bible, and began to read from it.

"After he, that is Jesus, had ended all his sayings in the hearing of the people, he entered Capernaum. The sayings," the chaplain explained, "refer to Luke's version of the Sermon on the Mount. At the very heart of this collection of Jesus' teachings is a passage which says, '... Love your enemies, do good to those who hate you, bless those who curse you. Pray for those who abuse you. To him who strikes you on the cheek, offer the other also...' 'As you wish that men would do to you, do so to them...' Now you can understand, can't you that this kind of teaching would not be popular? People were looking for a Messiah, a powerful warrior who would lead them in a successful revolt against mighty Rome. Jesus' teaching, 'Be merciful, even as your Father is merciful' must have sounded impractical to the people who remembered Sepphoris. Let me get back to the lesson:"

"Now a Centurion had a slave who was dear to him, who was sick and at the point of death. When he heard of Jesus, he sent to him elders of the Jews, asking him to come and heal his slave. Isn't that amazing," the chaplain interrupted the reading again.

"First it's amazing that an officer of the occupation cared anything at all about his slave. They were so abundant in the ancient world they could be simply replaced. Slave markets were common and the price of even a good one was embarrassingly cheap. From the very beginning we know this centurion to be an unusual man, of feelings and deep compassion. He not only cared about his slave, but he wants to get help so that he could be restored to health."

"Then did you hear the phrase, 'he heard of Jesus…'? Who told him about Jesus? Can't you imagine people would have said, 'his sort would never be interested in Jesus? He's a worshipper of Mars. His allegiance and obedience belong to Caesar.' But someone told this centurion something about Jesus. That's what excites me about these short services we share together. My task is to share the Word with you, believing it is going to go somewhere. Like ripples on a pond, you will share it with someone, who will share it with someone else. That's the truly amazing thing in this verse because it is Jewish elders who approach Jesus on behalf of a Roman. It's the kind of situation that experts agree would never happen with all that prejudice, bitterness and misunderstanding. Look how far off the text I got!"

"…they besought him earnestly, saying 'He is worthy to

have you do this for him, for he loves our nation, and he built us our synagogue.' For cryin' out loud, here is more of the puzzle: he's a soldier – an officer – a Roman leader who loves Israel! No one wanted to be assigned to this hateful, stubborn, and belligerent place. But wonder of wonders, he even builds a synagogue for them. Of course Jesus responded immediately and headed for the man's house. Here, let me read the rest of the story, 'He had gone a very short distance when the Centurion sent other messengers – this time friends – saying, 'Lord, do not trouble yourself, for I am not worthy to have you come under my roof; therefore I did not presume to come to you. But say the word, and let my servant be healed. For I am a man set under authority, with soldiers under me; I say to one, 'Go,' and he goes; and to another , 'Come,' and he comes; and to my slave, 'Do this," and he does it'. When Jesus heard this he marveled at him, and turned and said to the multitude that followed him, 'I tell you, not even in Israel have I found such faith.'"

"Notice what the Centurion understood that all the others had missed. This Roman officer clearly understood the authority of Jesus. He was absolutely convinced of the power of just the word of Jesus: '…but say the word and let my servant be healed.' I'll bet he had not studied the book of Genesis when God spoke the word of creation and there was light and the rest of creation. His study of philosophy had been limited at best, but looking at his own life, he began to put it together. He knew that his own word had authority. He would speak and the soldiers, slaves, or people around him would move into action. He understood that the word of Jesus had far greater power. He had faith potential."

# THE CORRUPTION OF FATHER MIKE

"I'm convinced that many of us in our own daily lives have the potential for bringing insights, clues, and understandings that can be used not just for our own growth and development, but primarily as a means of blessing and help to others. I'm also convinced because I have heard the lame excuses so often, 'Oh I really don't know anything about religion or miracles.' 'The only time I heard the Lord's name growing up was as profanity.' 'It seems like a fairy tale.' But I want to tell you this evening, you have already experienced the miracle of a new heart in your own chest."

"When a person is born, that person gets a new heart. Before the time of birth, you had a simple heart that had two chambers that just circulated your mom's blood which was oxygenated in her lungs. But at the time of your birth big changes occurred; that simple two chamber heart turned into a complex four chamber pump. The doctor swatted your cute little behind which made you gasp, and your own lungs filled with air. That new heart immediately pumped the blood to your lungs, where it was oxygenated, and then to every cell in your tiny body for nourishment. If that is not a miracle, I don't know one. With a word, God created you mysteriously. And the soldier knew that with a word, God through Jesus, could heal his servant."

"The response of Jesus was shocking, and completely unexpected: 'I tell you not even in Israel have I found such faith.' Remember, Israel was the land of faith. These were people of faith; their ancestor was Abraham, the father of the faith for goodness sake. The disciples were not commended for their great faith, nor were the priests or other holy folks, just the soldier, who understood that a word of authority was enough."

"So, how is your heart tonight? Can you dedicate yourself and what you bring to this moment, to be a channel of God's grace to a hurting world? I promise if you can there will be surprises. I promise you that God can repair your hurts, and use your life in a way you never imagined, to be an instrument of his grace. I promise you that he will take even the smallest faith and help to grow it. He will commend it – confirm it, -and expand your faith as a means of blessing others. Never forget that one day Jesus stopped the multitudes that followed him and said to them, 'I tell you that not even in Israel have I found such faith.' Friends, you have that kind of great faith potential! Now will you join me in the Coventry Cathedral Prayer?"

As Mike looked at his hand he was shocked to see his card crumpled in a fist, tight with tension.

He listened to the invitation to receive Holy Communion, and to the instructive prayer that accompanied it. The men stood to form a line to receive the sacrament. For once Mike was glad to be at the end. It gave him some time to try to pull himself together, He listened to the chaplain's words as the bread and cups were distributed. "Be assured of this: God loves you; God forgives you; God has a holy plan for you, and even now equips you with faith." The line continued to shuffle forward. "The past never has the last word; the powers of evil will never write the final chapter of history. Thanks be to God, who gives us the victory through our Lord, Jesus Christ." Mike was almost there. "Ask, and it will be given you; seek and you will find…" Mike picked up a small portion of bread. "Knock, and it will be opened to you," the chaplain was looking into his eyes as a tear traced down Mikes cheek.

# THE CORRUPTION OF FATHER MIKE

He was right behind Sergeant White as they were leaving the mess tent, when Mike heard the Chaplain's voice, "Hey John, hold on a minute." Obviously they knew one another well enough to be on a first name basis. As the Chaplain joined them he said to Sergeant White, "Sounds like you guys have had quite a couple days."

The Sergeant replied, "That was as fierce as I've ever seen. Artillery saved our asses for sure, and this guy," he nudged Mike with his elbow, "carried the heavy work."

Mike's weak smile was an attempt to control the scream that wanted to escape. "It wasn't that much," was all he could let out.

The Sergeant declared, "Yeah, not much; but enough to get a field promotion, and a recommendation from Blount for a Bronze Star!" That was the first Mike had heard of a medal.

"Wow, no wonder you are rattled today," the chaplain said reassuringly. "I had only heard the one-sided numbers." His hand rested on Mike's shoulder. "This job is like changing the baby's diaper. It's a shitty job, but someone has got to do it. If you think about all the men's lives you must have saved, it might help put a positive spin on it." He shrugged. "I know that sounds weak, so if you want to talk with me, you can find me at the M.A.S.H. unit right over there." He pointed to a tent complex. "What's your name, son?"

"Mike O'Malley, sir. There is one thing you can do for me, since you offered. Both Sergeant White and I have sort of abused our cards. I'd like to say we got most of the prayer out of them. Do you think we might have a replacement? I'll try to take better care of mine." Two cards were fished out of the chaplain's shirt pocket.

"Do you guys have time for a quick prayer?" he asked. While they bowed where they stood, the Chaplain grasped a hand of each, saying, "Heavenly Father in this place of struggle, we thank you for your constant care for us, and ask that you would give us tonight quiet minds that are eager to seek your way; memories which are strong to hold what is useful, and release of that which is not. Grant us wills that are dedicated to obey, hearts which are surrendered to love, and lives which are committed to serve where needed. We are confident in your care for us and pray for our brothers at arms who also stand in need of your protection, in Jesus' name." All three of them said, "Amen." As Mike walked back to his tent, he could finally take a deep breath without feeling like he was about to bawl.

In the following three weeks he made four more trips up to the top of 266, outpost 11. It was almost comical. I shoot at you, you shoot at me, then you call in artillery and I move off the top a ways, then I call in artillery and you move off the top a ways, then I shoot at you. All this time the peace talks were going on in Panmunjom; the main sticking point was the repatriation of Chinese and North Korean prisoner who didn't want to go back to North Korea. So it was the Old Baldy two-step, until the Chinese wanted to send a message to the peace talks.

Mike was in the second of four trucks grinding their way up the hill. This was his sixth trip, and he had the route pretty well memorized. They came around a shoulder and suddenly the truck in front exploded! A Chinese Howitzer had been hidden in a gully about a hundred yards off the road. At that distance it would have been hard for him to miss. The round hit the truck driver's door, blowing the cab all to pieces. The bed of the truck was thrown over, spilling nearly fifty men and their equipment. Mike saw most of them crawl for cover, but three or four lay motionless.

The round that hit his truck took out the rear wheels, sending the bed and all the passengers into the air. The truck slowly turned over into the ditch. Mike had tried to hold onto the Browning with his right hand, but lost track of the ammo case. In his effort to stay upright, he had held onto the rail around the bed with his left hand, and felt his shoulder pop with a vicious pain; then he couldn't move his arm, and fell with the rest of the passengers.

There was another explosion as a round hit the truck behind them; this one was a direct hit on the bed where all those men were standing. The casualties were nearly total. Mike was trying to scuttle around the wreckage, pulling men into a semblance of cover, and yelling for others to get off the road, or stay down, or look out! The fourth truck was careening in reverse to stand clear of the enemy fire.

It took three hours to get the wounded back to the base camp, and another two hours before a doctor could get to Mike's shoulder. He was hungry and in considerable pain, finally, in the Mobile Army Surgical Hospital tent it was determined that he had dislocated his shoulder and probably torn the rotator cuff all to hell. They would send him to an Orthopedist in Ch'orwan. All the cots were full of the wounded, so Mike stood by a heavy steel book case, while they were fitting him in a sling. Looking at the large collection of available books, he wondered, "Who would read the Smithsonian Annual?" The four shelves were filled with the bound volumes.

There was a sudden bump on the tent top as a heavy object tore through. It hit the floor about three feet from where Mike was standing. Startled, he wondered how it had missed all of the cots, but then he noticed it was smoking, the fuse of the projectile was still active! Someone shouted "Grenade!" Later, he would wonder how in the world he managed to think about his action, because he is still sure that it happened instinctively. He grabbed the corner of the bookcase with his good hand and yanked. As the bookcase tipped, several men scrambled out of the way. Mike kept pushing as it gained momentum, and then he sort of rode it onto the smoking object. He didn't hear the explosion.

When he regained consciousness, he was lying in the road with a number of others. The tent was in shambles, but still standing. There was lots of frantic activity to treat those who had shrapnel wounds, but surprisingly, there seemed to be no fatalities. Mike became aware of blood on his face and chest. But it was not serious. He was amazed at the quiet; then he realized it was because he couldn't hear anything, not a whisper.

A corpsman knelt beside him and started cleaning the wound on his forehead. With forceps he pulled a sliver of metal from the wound. Mike growled, "I can't hear," and the medic nodded his understanding. Another piece of metal was pulled out of his chest before the medic turned attention to his ears. A sticky mucous was on the sides of his face. As it was wiped clean the medic's mouth moved but Mike had no clue as to what he was saying. Finally, the young man took a pad of paper and quickly wrote, "drums burst, be O.K." Then he was gone to help others. Mike thought in silence, "Well, I'm only a little hurt. We can handle this." He tried his best to remember the *Te Deum*.

He was given a box of K rations on the truck taking him back to Ch'orwan. There he was given stitches on his forehead, chest and three wounds on his arm that hadn't been noticed. They also gave him another box, and a seat on an east bound air freighter that refueled at Hickam in Hawaii, and eventually arrived at McCord Air Force Base in Washington. Madigan Hospital at Fort Lewis would be his home while the shoulder healed and the ear damage could be assessed and treated. The injuries were serious enough to end his military service. It happened so quickly that Mike had a challenge following his exit. He was pretty sure that his duffle was with him, but he wondered if the Browning ever made it back to the armory.

A basketball player sized Captain came into his hospital room holding a note, which said, "Hi Mike, I'm Father Jennings, Chaplain here at Fort Lewis. I got a note from Father Blake, saying that I should treat you like a hero. I answered him saying that's how we treat all our men, because they are." Mike smiled, liking the Chaplain's sense of humor immediately. Or maybe it was the painkillers he had been on for three days since the surgery. When the doctors got into his shoulder they found that the bone had been broken along with the rotator tear. He would be in a cast for at least a month. Then there would be another month of physical therapy, and then he would find out how serious his hearing loss would be. The prospects were that he would be discharged by Christmas.

"May I contact anyone for you, to tell them you are O.K.?" the chaplain's note asked. When Mike tried to talk it just sounded like a roar in his head. But he tried anyway, "No one. My folks aren't much around."

The chaplain scribbled, "Fr. Blake said you wrote no letters home, didn't receive any either. No one?"

Mike shook his head.

"I'll introduce you to some new friends as soon as you can get around. O.K.?" The chaplain had a very pleasant smile for a man as tall as a tree. He gave Mike a book of prayers before he left.

The process of healing usually happens while we are busy doing something else. In Mike's case it was the only thing happening. The doctors had inserted a foam plug in each ear to hold in the antibiotics and promote healing. He did read the *Count of Monte Cristo*, while he was in a silent bed for two weeks. He knew he was improving when he read *Gulliver's Travels* when at last he was allowed to go to the silent dining room in between silent naps. The Chaplain looked in on him a few times, but there was no conversation, just notebook exchange with a roaring response. Mike tried to make himself talk very quietly, but it was still garbled noise in his head.

On the Monday before Thanksgiving he was fit with a third kind of hearing aid that was a big improvement. He could hear voices fairly well, and background noise was only a bit irritating. He felt he could adequately carry on a conversation. His arm was still in a sling, but that too was manageable. His duffle bag had joined him, complete with his wallet still having money in it. Sergeant White had tucked in the Browning's canvas bag as a souvenir, saying that it was being returned for cleaning. A card with his contact information said simply, "A promise made is a debt unpaid! John"

An attractive Lieutenant from the Office of Separation brought him his Honorable Discharge for Medical Purposes document; along with it there was his promotion to Corporal certificate and several honors: A Good Conduct medal, which almost everyone receives, a Purple Heart, which most are fortunate enough not to earn, a Soldier's Medal for Heroism and a Bronze Star for his actions on Hill 266, an Army Commendation and a Silver Star for his actions in the defense of the medical unit;. There was finally a Japanese Commendation for public service awarded by the Yokosuka Police. When seen all together he realized what a packed eighteen months he had lived, and wondered what the months ahead would bring. He was given an 80% disability rating, to be reviewed annually, so he would get some kind of money to live on. Mike also received all his back pay since Yokosuka, and the information that he had been awarded full G.I. Bill benefits for his full three year enlistment.

# Discharged to a New life

The Greyhound picked him up at the main gate bus stop. For $6.50 he could ride to Portland. As he crossed the Columbia River, and saw the "Welcome to Oregon" sign, a wave of joy surged through Mike. There had been no farewell when he left, and would be no fanfare when he came home. But it did feel like a homecoming. The familiar sights were comforting. The cab driver that took him from the bus station to his N.E. Union Ave home was less than talkative in the run-down neighborhood. Again to Mike, it felt like a homecoming. He was pretty sure no one would be there to greet him, but he was anxious to see his bedroom again.

On his bed was a neat pile of mail. As Mike shuffled through it, there was much to discard, but he found a letter from his wrestling coach, which was a nice "take it easy" sort of letter. It was a thoughtful connection. Another was from Brad Phillips, wishing him safety and health in the Korean War. That also was pleasing to Mike that his wrestling nemesis actually had a thought about him. There was a flier from the school class ring folks. Mike's lack of funds then had precluded his purchase. Now he had some cash, but little interest in ordering one. There were two letters from Ernie. The first one written from the juvenile detention center, was a short request for return mail, telling Mike a bit of an excuse for the gun shop burglary. The second one was dated just a month ago, written from the Oregon Correctional Institute, a fancy name for a first time offender's prison. Ernie had a favor to ask, but would do it only over the phone. He gave Mike some contact information, and little motivation to do it.

The top letter was from the University of Portland, with a hand written address. Mike had no way of knowing that his life was about to take a major shift. Curiously he opened the letter from Fr. Preston James. Mike thought the names could be interchanged. It read: "Dear Mr. O'Malley. Please let me introduce myself. I am Fr. Preston James, Registrar at the University of Portland. I hope you are familiar with the school and have, perhaps, included it in your possible future matriculation." Mike stopped to wonder what that might mean and was fairly suspicious it was not good. "The reason I am contacting you today is in response to a request by one of our alumni, Fr. C. C. Blake, who you met earlier this year in Korea. He has informed me of your outstanding character and bravery, and believes you might be a scholastic candidate once your war injuries are healed. Ordinarily we accept applications for study grants much earlier in the year because applying allows you to define who you are and to clarify where you are going with your life. It is a process of self-discovery and self-definition. It is time consuming and laborious, but the rewards outweigh the effort required".

"It is Fr. Blake's hope that this offer might work in reverse for you, allowing you to attend classes here as you discover the possible applications for your education, and the plethora of destinations your education might take you. You have already defined the quality of your character the hard way. That being said, there is a time urgency to this offer, for we have a winter quarter beginning in just a month. If you so choose, you are welcome to call me as soon as possible to arrange a class schedule for you under a Gilman Scholarship award, which along with tuition, covers the expenses of books and study materials required by the instructors. It will be an honor to speak with you soon. Yours in Advent anticipation. Father Preston James."

"Holy Shit!" Mike thought as he read the letter again. "Holy Shit!" College!

He walked to the dime store to get some paper, envelopes, and stamps so he could write back to Ernie, and Sergeant White. He just needed some time to focus on the offer. By the time he had made it almost back home, he thought, "What's to consider? This seems too good to be true! So I don't know what I want to be when I grow up. I'm only nineteen! I'll work it out." He made an appointment to see Father James in the morning, hoping his mom would let him use the car tonight to get some decent clothes, and to drive to the campus. He was grateful for the stash of cash he had.

At 10:00 a.m. the next morning he was directed to Father James' office. Wearing new shoes, black slacks, a gray shirt and tie and a Herringbone sport coat, he looked nothing at all like a corporal recently home from battle. There were several official forms to be filled out, but first Fr. James wanted to ask him some questions, "What are some of the subjects you would like to begin with? What academic goals do you have?"

With a relaxed smile, Mike answered, "To tell you the truth, sir, I haven't ruled anything out. I've dreamed of being a wrestling coach, or a teacher. I can't see myself as a banker or businessman. I'll bet there are hundreds of jobs I would love to do, so any study that would make that happen is great for me." He reflected for a moment. "The last sermon I heard Fr. Blake give, caught my attention for a lot of reasons. He said we are great faith people if we receive a new heart, one to serve and help others. That struck a chord in me. I have no idea what God wants to do with me, but I'll bet with your help we'll find out." Then with a final thought he added, "I suppose at this late date, most of your classes are full. I would be happy to be put in any that needs more attendance. I'm hoping I can be around for a while. That will give me time to be selective."

"Fr. Blake said that you were a most humble hero. Are your injuries healing?" He had actually heard all that he needed to place their plan in motion.

"The shoulder will take a while to regain range of motion and strength; the doctors say that my hearing may return some. Right now I am dependent on these hearing aids, and they also tell me that the bad memories will lessen."

"Was that when you earned the silver star?"

Mike was surprised at the information that had been shared about him. "No, sir. My first taste of combat was terrible; that's where the bronze star was earned. I fired more than 300 rounds of thirty-ought-six bullets into a trench-full of Chinese soldiers. I killed more than we could count. Some, two with one bullet. Those are the images that I try not to see every night. The doctors say it is shell-shock, or post-battle stress, and will eventually go away." He shook his head, admitting that he didn't know the answer, if there might be one. "I just want to help people."

"Have you ever thought of law enforcement?" An idea had

just occurred to the registrar.

"Well, sir," Mike shook his head a bit. "I was Military Police for about nine months in Japan. In fact, I received a commendation award from them. But I think I would feel better doing something that doesn't require brute force. I'm a little too good at that." His smile was genuine.

"Are you going to try to find a job while you are also doing school work?" Mike could read nothing behind the question.

"I have some G.I. Bill tuition credit, but nothing but my disability checks to pay for rent and expenses, so I guess the answer is, yes sir, I will need to find a job.'"

"I'll need to look into this before I can offer it to you, along with a scholarship, but we are always in need of good security guards here, someone who can check doors at night, and quiet occasional noisy groups. If there is ever a medical emergency, security is usually the first one there; so basic first aid training is required. It only pays minimum salary, but you will have lots of study time. Might you be interested in that?"

"Yes, sir. This sounds better all the time."

"Then let's see if we can tie some of this down before I take it to the trustees. As a basic freshman package how about..." his eyes were studying a list of classes. "Monday, Wednesday and Friday let's have you do American History, Modern Literature, and Economic Geography. There is only one paper required for each of those. And for Tuesday and Thursdays let's add the New Testament Introduction, and Church History. Both of those are fun with more quizzes than tests or papers." He studied the list. "Mr. O'Malley, I know you have been through some very challenging times recently. By comparison, this will be a walk in the park. I am serving you up a different challenge. If you can do at least passing work on this study schedule plus working as security guard, we will continue the Gilman Scholarship for another year. Is that a fair offer?"

"It is more than fair, sir. I'd call it graciously generous." There were tears in his eyes as he held out a handshake to seal the deal. Fr. James was assured that this was indeed the man to receive all the help this school could give. Mike was given a list of books to read before the new quarter began. The note he carried to the bookstore authorized them to give him the books at no charge. It would be the first Bible he ever owned.

When he got home he had a lot to tell his mom. The lifeless little house was in sharp contrast with his feelings. It occurred to him that there were no Christmas decorations of any sort in the house. They were drinking a pot of tea when he asked her about that. She told him, "I really haven't had much use for that stuff this year. Hank (Mike's dad) got his self arrested in Kansas. He got caught having sex with a 15 year old prostitute in a Truck Stop. I guess it's going to be three or four years before he gets out, and then it will be to no driving job. I'm just plain tired of carrying this place." She looked weary to the bone. "Christmas lights don't mean much this year."

"Well I have some news that might put a little sparkle in the day." He wasn't about to tell her of the cash or back paychecks that he had in his room, but the conversation at University of Portland was first-class news.

She only asked, "Are you going to be living here or get your own place?" Mike could see what had always been the case; she was so beat down that not even great news would lift her spirit.

"We'll see what the trustees think about it, but if I get the scholarship and the guard job, I will find a place I can rent within walking distance of the school. That way I won't need the expense of a car." To him the news was worthy of Christmas lights and a tinsel tree. He showed her the pile of books he had to start reading.

"Then you better get started," was her only comment.

Mike went to his room to write an exuberant thank you note to Fr. Blake. "Your influence is truly world- wide," he wrote to his favorite chaplain. "I'll keep you in touch with our progress." Then he wrote notes to Sergeant White and Ernie, telling them how welcome their mail had been to him, and wished them a Merry Christmas. He thought it best to hold off on the scholastic announcement. There would be plenty of time for that later.

"Now which one of these textbooks shall I read first?" he asked himself. Choosing the Bible he turned to the Gospel of Matthew, saying, "Let's begin correctly." So began a learning marathon. Books, Mike came to understand, were treasure troves of information. Dig well enough and they would yield their abundance. On December 14th Fr. James phoned to say that the trustees had approved all aspects of their proposal. As soon as Mike could come in for the necessary paperwork and orientation, he could begin drawing pay.

There was one more surprise that filled Mike's cup to overflowing. When Marty Powers, the Security Chief was giving him the cook's tour of the campus, which doors had to be locked and checked through the night, which parking spaces were assigned, and which rooms were occupied by staff, he guided Mike to the fourth floor of the men's dorm. In a gable, there was an empty single room, which had been assigned for

Mike's use. It had been determined that having a security staff person in residence was a beneficial thing for the welfare of the students. Along with it came a $100 per month cafeteria allotment. He could not be more prepared to do his very best!

When Mike shared this final part of the plan with his mom, her only response was, "You better not fail. There are a lot of folks depending on you." Curiously, Mike had not even given the idea of failure a thought.

# Student at the University of Portland

Chief Powers was trying to hide the exuberance he was feeling for having staff at last. The security service to the campus had been staggering along with his time and a patchwork of temporary and volunteer help. Mike was the real deal. In fact, were you to ask Marty, Mike should be the chief, yet he had accepted the graveyard shift, the most unpleasant. He took the lock-up duties and then checked the campus every hour all night long. It was beyond the understanding of the Chief how this could be called fair.

If you were to ask Mike, however, he would give a different point of view: "Wow, I get to show up for work to lock three buildings, then I get to study for forty-five minutes; check the buildings again and study for forty-five minutes. I get paid for a dime's worth of work and a dollar's worth of study. It sure works for me." He had discovered that the weight room was available as he unlocked the doors at 7 a.m. He could work out for half an hour before grabbing breakfast and then a few hours of sleep. He chose a locker where a gym bag with a sweatshirt, gym shoes and a towel could be kept. The shoulder was getting stronger all the time.

One night as he was locking the music building, he heard

# THE CORRUPTION OF FATHER MIKE

the most beautiful sound he had ever heard. He moved toward the sound and found the glee choir rehearsing for the Christmas concert. When Marty asked if he could work early to help with the large crowd coming to hear the concert, Mike was only politely eager to comply. He helped with parking, guiding folks to the auditorium, then listening with rapt attention to the musical account of the birth of Jesus. The Christmas story had never been so clearly and beautifully presented to him. To his complete joy, there were three nights to repeat the duty. He smiled knowing that he was getting paid to do what he would gladly pay to witness.

At the Union Pacific train station, while Mike was being inspired, a sinister scam was taking place. An attractive girl was struck with a wood rasp, first on the shoulder and then on the side of her head. When she was sure no one was looking she screamed to get attention, and carefully "fell" down the stairs of a passenger car. Helpful travelers hurried to her aid, and a conveniently available Portland Police officer took photos of her bleeding shoulder and head, and witness accounts of the accident.

From Christmas to the fourth of January, the campus was closed. Most of the students were away; only a handful were at the cafeteria for meals. Mike asked if he could get a sandwich to take to work on the night shift. From then on there was a paper sack with a sandwich and an apple, or some other treat, waiting for him at lunch. The schedule was working; he finished reading the textbooks for the winter quarter.

On New Year's Eve a prominent Judge was in the Sheraton Hotel, hosting a political fund-raiser. At 2:00 a.m., when all the party goers had left, the door to his room opened and a lovely woman wearing very little, walked up to him in an affectionate manner. The Judge tried to fend her away, but a flash of a camera caught him in a most compromised situation. The woman quickly hurried out of the room.

Mike awoke well before dawn crept into his room. He went down the hall to the bathroom to shower and shave. With fresh new pants and shirt, he decide to reread the first three chapters of the textbook before going to breakfast. Was he eager to be a freshman student? "Damn right!" His first class was Modern Literature and he chose a seat on the aisle about mid way back. He was ready!

"Good morning, I'm Dr. Jenny Crumb. It's good to see those of you who were in Classic Literature, and now those of you joining the class." Her opening description of literature contended that all good writing has been like love letters, some ardent and some in anguish, to unseen readers. "Let me ask you," she raised a question that would be of interest to almost all of the students, "have you received a love letter recently? Well then, have you written a love letter?" There was a general chuckle from the students.

"We are going to try an experiment this quarter. I'm giving you an assignment this morning, on our first gathering, of writing a love letter to yourself." Again the chuckle rippled, but this time a bit louder. "Yes, it sounds unusual, and I agree, it is. I am asking you to write, daily, the most exceptional idea that you receive, from whatever source; that's part one. I would like you to write how you react or feel about that idea; that's step two. Those compiled writings will account for one third of your grade; isn't that fun? Yes, that is equal to a midterm, and it is very subjective . It is also Modern Literature."

Up on Barber Blvd. a grocery truck was being pulled over by three armed men, who forced the driver out and drove away. They required the restaurant that sorely needed the shipment for their evening meal, to pay a "finder's fee."

In the Geographic Economy class, the professor asked a discussion question: "Do you believe the current growth trend of the U.S. economy will continue?" After several optimistic answers, Mike offered, "I believe if the present trend of failing American steel mills, along with increased foreign automobile imports continues, it will cause a decline in our economy." The professor marked him as a student with understanding and interest.

In the Multnomah County Building Department, a Permit Specialist with excessive gambling debts to Paul Levine, was denied for the third time an exemption request, halting the completion of a multimillion dollar shopping center development owned by Antonio Caesar.

In the American History class, Mike was the only student to raise his hand. When the professor called on him, he answered, "Washington's December 25th crossing of the Delaware River." "That is correct Mr. ....O'Malley. Thank you for reading the assignment."

Just west of Parkrose on N.E. Lombard, a school bus struck a car driven by a young woman. The car careened out of control, finally rolling in the ditch. The driver had extensive injuries to her shoulder and head. Fortunately a Portland Police officer was nearby to take photos and interview witnesses.

Mike took a fresh spiral bound notebook and wrote on the cover, "A Love Letter to Mike." On the first page he wrote:

"Father Franks said, 'A day that begins with gratitude is a

day that you will be able to fill with positive progress. When you are sincerely appreciative of where you are and what you have, you will greatly expand your own possibilities. Begin with a thankful thought. Connect yourself with the abundance that is all around you. There is always something for which you can be sincerely thankful. The simple act of being thankful ignites a productive momentum in your world. By focusing your thoughts on the positive aspects of your life, you cause their influence to grow. Be grateful, and your gratitude happily creates even more things in your life for which you can be grateful. It's a snowball effect. The appreciation for what you have gives more value to all that you are. The blessings you enjoy are blessings precisely because you see them as such. Tap into the great reservoir of real value that is available to you. Live with gratitude, and you will create even more reasons to be thankful.'

"How do I feel about that? Like a very blessed young man who has received far more than he deserves!"

In NE Portland a Loomis truck pulled into the parking lot shortly after the bank opened. One courier moved to the back door, while the other was on guard. When the door swung open two men stepped out of the bank with shotguns. Both the driver and the one carrying two bags of money were hit. The shooters jumped in a car and sped away. Within minutes they were confronted in a house on the outskirts, and fatally shot by a Portland Police detective; the money was never recovered.

Mike realized that his preparation for the classes made the material clear and practically easy! It was a discovery he would maintain for the next five years.

In the office of Antonio Caesar, a man was trying to explain why he was late with a loan payment. "You knew there was interest to pay," a rough looking man said. "But I didn't know it was due weekly!" There was genuine fear in his voice. "You got two days to come up with the payment or we take over your business, understand?" "I don't know if I can get the money that quick." "Two days or don't come back; we'll find you!" The threat was understood.

On Tuesday afternoon Mike felt more rested. He was ready for his introduction to the New Testament. Father Lopez had a huge smile that compensated for his thick Spanish accent. Mike tried to take good notes:

"'Synoptic' is a word made up of two other words, 'together,' and 'to see.' It means to be able to be seen together. Mark's Gospel has been seen as the earliest written, because it is the most urgent, with no birth narrative, or developed Resurrection account. Mark's arrangement of events are mirrored by both Matthew and Luke, while the other two add material special to their particular readers. Matthew has a Hebrew emphasis, and Luke is written for a Greek audience. Mark also contains information that implies an eye-witness. Papias, a second century historian, identifies Mark as Simon Peter's interpreter, and the Gospel as basically Peter's preaching material."

"Who is Mark? There is considerable information about him in the New Testament. John Mark was the son of a wealthy lady of Jerusalem named Mary, who owned a house with an upper room – the location of the Last Supper, and an early gathering place for the infant Church (Acts 12:12). He was also the nephew of Barnabas, who took him along on Paul's first missionary journey. Mark returned home prematurely, causing

Paul's refusal to allow him on the second journey. Ultimately, Barnabas and Mark sail to Cyprus, and very possibly into a mission to Asia Minor (the churches of the Revelation). However, reconciliation eventually happens, for when Paul writes the letter to the Colossians from prison, Mark is with him, and Paul includes him as his fellow worker."

"Mark's Gospel can be divided into 105 sections (pericopes). Of these, 93 occur in Matthew, and 81 in Luke. Of Mark's 105, only four are not found in the other two. Or said more finely, Mark has 661 verses; Matthew 1,068, and Luke 1,149. Matthew reproduces no less than 606 of Mark's verses, and Luke reproduces 320. There are only 24 verses in the whole of Mark not included in the other two."

"It is important to point out here that the verses drawn from Mark are almost entirely material dealing with the *events* of Jesus' life. There is an additional 200 verses common to both Matthew and Luke that tell us not what Jesus did, but what he *said*. This has led scholars to believe that either they were copying from some common source book, or one of them was copying the other. For those who believe there was a common source book the letter Q *(German word "quelle" for source)* represents this teaching handbook or earliest collection of writings."

"One more thing to note before we get to the characteristics of Mark's Gospel; in its original form, Mark stops at Mark 16:8. In the most ancient manuscript verses 9 – 20 are not included. The style of the Greek contained in those verses implies that they could not have been written by the same person. What happened? We can only speculate. Since the common dating of the original writing is as early as A.D. 45, this premature conclusion may have been brought about by the death of Peter. It could also indicate the dynamic days of the emergence of the Church, as Mark is carried along into the missionary movement to originate congregations of the Mediterranean world."

"What to watch for as you read it:

1.) This is the nearest thing we can get to a picture of the life of Jesus. It is Mark's delight to tell it simply and in the most dramatic way.

2.) Mark never forgot the divine side of Jesus. He begins his work with these words: "The beginning of the gospel of Jesus Christ, the Son of God." He leaves no room for misunderstanding. Again and again, he reports the awe of those who were touched by Jesus, or the amazement he created in others. To Mark, Jesus was not just one of us; he was God with us, constantly moving people to wonder and awe with his words and deeds.

3.) At the same time, no gospel shows us a more human picture of Jesus. His account of Jesus lets us see a man who is compassionate, righteously angry, amazed at their unbelief, hungry and thirsty. When Jesus looked at the rich young ruler, he loved him. The sheer humanity of Jesus in Mark's picture brings him very near to us.

4.) There is intimate detail to some of Mark's accounts. When Matthew and Luke write about Jesus taking the little child and setting him in their midst, Mark adds, "And taking him in his arms, he said to them…" (9:36.) Or the feeding of the five thousand, only Mark explains that they sat in hundreds and fifties, looking like vegetable gardens (6:40.) Or when Mark tells the story of the stilling of the storm, he remembers that Jesus was asleep on the stern, "his head on a pillow." That one phrase makes the picture personal and vivid before our eyes.

5.) Mark is very fond of the words "immediate," and "straightaway." He uses them nearly thirty times. Some stories march along with dignity, but Mark's has a near frantic pace to get it told.

6.) His style of writing can best be described as immature, frequently connecting phrases together with an "and." In chapter three for example, in the Greek, there are 34 clauses or sentences introduced that way with just one principle verb. It is the way an eager child would tell it.

7.) Finally, Mark often gives us the Aramaic words which Jesus used. To Jairus' daughter, Jesus said, "Talitha cumi" (5:41) To the deaf man, he said, Ephphatha!" (7:34.) The dedicated gift is "Corba" (7:11) In the garden of prayer, Jesus says, "Abba, Father," (14:36.) And from the cross, Jesus spoke, "Eloi, Eloi, lema sabachthani?" (15:34.) There are times when Peter could hear again the very dear sound of Jesus' voice, and could not help passing it on to Mark in the account he would record."

In room 419 of the Benson Hotel, a drugged Rotarian was being stripped to pose for the camera. He had been slipped a Mickey at the bar; now unconscious and naked he could not prevent the young woman from crawling under him. "O.K. Lee, now hook your leg over him. Make it look real. Now push his face toward me. Yeah, he'll pay for these." Blackmail is a dirty business.

In Notebook, Mike wrote: *"Every success is first a success of the imagination. What wonderful pathways will you dare to imagine?"*

*How do I feel about that? 'Like someone awakening in a strange land. It is a completely unfamiliar thought that I might 'dare to imagine.'*

# THE CORRUPTION OF FATHER MIKE

As his Church History introduction was concluding the professor said:

Notebook: *"Those who achieve the most do not see themselves competing. They see themselves serving. If you wish to make clear and unmistakable progress, be of service. If you seek to create great value, be of service. When your strategy is to grab all you can, as quickly as you can, you will be met with debilitating opposition. When your strategy is to be of genuine service, your support will run far and wide. It is foolish to think that you can fight against the world. True success comes when you choose to work for the world. At any age, in any condition, for every circumstance, there is much you can give to life. Look for what you can offer, and there is much that you will find. Choose always, at every opportunity to be of service."*

How do I feel about that? Refreshed, like a cup of stream water, clear and clean.

As Mike found the rhythm of his academic world, security, with lots of reading, a short morning rest, then classes each day, study and rest again before clocking in at the security office, each day of the week passed effortlessly.

He had no way of knowing that not far away was another rhythm, a criminal one of fraud, extortion, theft and violence. The two rhythms would collide in the future. But just not today.

Econ Notebook:) *"What you do not know, you can learn. What you do not have, you can work to create or acquire. The experience you seek is unfolding in every moment. Let life flow as it will, and you move toward your dream. What you see as a challenge is the opportunity for which we have been waiting. Now is your turn to achieve. The time you invest in meaningful effort will produce rewards that continue to grow more valuable. And you will fill your life with a richness that can never be taken away."*

*How do I feel? I am coming to believe that I have expected too little from others, from life, and most definitely from myself!*

Mike was sitting in the security office reading tomorrow's assignment. The phone rang and an excited voice announced that a group of men were raiding the women's dormitory. In the background he could hear shouts and screams. Grabbing his two nightsticks, he loped the hundred yards across the quad.

As soon as he entered the dormitory, he could hear distraught voices from the second floor. He took the stairs, three at a time. The hallway had several young women pointing at the rooms at the far end of the hall. "There are several of them!" one woman announced. Mike moved carefully but very directly toward the problem.

Three young men with huge grins stepped out of a room on his left. In their hands were women's lingerie. "For cryin' out loud," he thought; "It's a damned panty raid!" Three men appeared from the right hand side of the hallway, also with their prizes. They all stopped dead still considering the alternatives before them.

Mike said, "Sit down and we can work this out."

The six saw only a minor obstacle, a security person with night sticks, so they chose to ignore him.

"Gentlemen, please don't make this worse than it needs to be. Sit down!" Mike directed.

One of the raiders said through a sneer, "Don't do anything with your little sticks that you'll regret. Get out of our way!" As he took a step forward the others followed his lead.

"Guys, this doesn't need to happen. Are any of you on a sports scholarship? I don't want to hurt you," Mike pleaded.

The six totally misunderstood his warning, so they took another step. Mike set his foot as a brace behind him, now sure that confrontation was eminent. They took one more hesitant step, then launched the attack at the security guard. The leader of the charge was the first one to fall. The sweeping nightstick took out his knee. In the next four seconds the other five all received repeated strikes; elbows, collar bones, wrists, shoulders, and a second knee were damaged. As Mike surveyed the writhing raiders, he asked one of the women to call the switchboard, and request ambulances to transfer these young men to the hospital. His reputation as a fierce man of peace had just become legend. Never again would the security guards be under-estimated. Mike was sure there would be a lot of paper-work and explanations for this encounter.

The phone call from the Provost's Office was no surprise. He was asked to meet with the Trustees to explain the incident. When the hour arrived, Mike faced the dour faced men feeling as though he was on trial, which he was. "Tell us your side of the account, Mr. O'Malley," they began. Mike assumed they had already heard another "side of the story."

"Sir, I responded to a call from the women's dorm logged in at 1010 p.m. It is a short distance from the security office, so I ran, following the screams to the second floor. The women pointed me to the end of the hallway, which had several distraught women pointing to the rooms being rifled."

One of the Trustees interrupted, "That's a pretty strong word."

"Perhaps, sir," Mike answered. "What would you call an uninvited group of men pawing through a woman's undergarments, selecting a fistful to keep as souvenirs?" When there was no response, he continued, "Three men came out of the room on the left side of the hallway, each holding women's panties; then three came out of the right, also carrying private garments. I asked them to sit down so we could handle the moment peacefully, rationally. They refused. I warned them not to move toward me; they chose not to heed that warning. I ask if they had sports scholarships that might be in jeopardy, and they rushed at me. I handled the situation, and then asked the women to call the switchboard for ambulances. That call is recorded at 10:17 p.m."

"Do you feel you used excessive force?" one of the men asked.

"No sir, I do not. I used just enough to maintain the safety of the women, to control the situation and cause no permanent injuries."

One of the Trustees said excitedly, "For God's sake, my son has a broken wrist. That seems excessive to me. Couldn't you have simply let them pass?"

"Yes sir, I could have done that," Mike answered thoughtfully.

"Good God, it was only panties," another murmured.

"Would it have been more appropriate if they were taking silver or gems?" Mike asked without being defensive. "Let me ask you," he continued, "If six men forced their way into your home, barged into your wife's room, your daughter's room, rummaging through their personal and private things, intent on taking them, would you want the police to simply let them run off into the night, enjoying their little prank?" When there was no answer, Mike added, "I think the question you might want to consider is: 'was my constraint in using a little force appropriate to the moment, when so much more

# THE CORRUPTION OF FATHER MIKE

was available.'" The ominous sound of that caused each man to consider their judgment. Finally, the Provost asked, "Is there anything more you would like us to know on this matter, Mr. O'Malley?"

"If you are asking me for an apology for hurting these men, you have it. I am very sorry for their pain. That surely was not my first choice as resolution, and I tried to avoid it as much as I could. If you are asking if I think I should lose my job over this, I would say that is up to you. If you are asking would I do it differently given a second chance, I would tell you flatly, 'No, I acted in complete accordance with my job description and the rules of this University.' Their injuries will heal. I hope their respect for other's property, and respect for authorities, will improve. I hope the women feel safe in their dorm. All in all, this was a painful but useful learning time for everyone." He had nothing more to add, and heard nothing more from the Provost.

Econ Notebook: *"There are lots of things you could have been, could have done, could have seen, could have known, and could have experienced. Yet nothing compares to the wondrous places you will go when you do what you know you can!"*

*How do I feel about that? Having sorrow for the past is of no value, but having confidence in my future potential is of great value.*

Literature Notebook: *"Be kind to yourself. The better you feel, the more value you can create for your world. Learn from your mistakes, but don't hound yourself relentlessly with them. Build for the future, but don't withhold from yourself the joys you can live right now. Treat yourself with kindness, courtesy, respect, and the highest of expectations, for life is as good as you choose to make it!"*

*How do I feel about that? If it is going to be, it's up to me!*

Church History Notebook: Augustine of Hippo (354 - 430) "You have made us for yourself, and our hearts are restless till they rest in you." Augustine's prayer could also be a commentary on his own life.

"Born at Tagaste in Algeria of a pagan father and a Christian mother, he was brought up in the Christian faith. A brilliant student, he planned to be a lawyer, and studied rhetoric at the University of Carthage. There, puzzled by the problem of evil, he rejected his childhood faith".

"His mother Monica, continued to pray for him. While teaching in Milan, Augustine came under the influence of Bishop Ambrose, and began to search for God. His crisis came when in the midst of a spiritual struggle, he heard a childish voice saying, 'Tolle, lege.' – 'Pick up and read.' He picked up the Bible, which he had formerly despised, and the words he read drew him to God."

"Within five years Augustine had become a bishop in his native North Africa. His spiritual writings – the autobiographical 'Confessions,' and the great theological work, 'City of God,' have become classics of the faith for all time."

"Augustine, The House of the Soul: 'O Lord, the house of my soul is narrow; enlarge it that you may enter in. It is ruinous, O repair it! It displeases your sight; I confess it, I know. But who shall cleanse it, to whom shall I cry but to you? Cleanse me from my secret faults, O Lord, and spare your servant from strange sins.'"

Mike really liked the New Testament class. Fr. Lopez always seemed to be overjoyed with the material, which Mike was hearing for the first time.

New Testament: The chubby priest clapped his hands and

said, "Now that we have looked at the Essential Gospel, let's look at Matthew, the Majestic Gospel. It's the next piece of the puzzle of the synoptic problem. We actually know little about the person Matthew. We can read of his call to discipleship in 9:9. We know that he was a tax gatherer, and must have therefore been a bitterly hated man, since the Jews hated those of their own nationality who entered the civil service of their conquerors. Tax collectors became wealthy in the abuse of power given them. Matthew would have been regarded as nothing less than a collaborator, and a traitor to his own people."

"Most of the men Jesus called were common fishermen. They would have had little skill or practice in the art of putting words together, writing them in a record. Matthew would have been an expert in that sort of craft. When Jesus called him from his customs duty, Matthew rose up and followed him, and left everything behind him, except his pen."

"There had to be generations of the development of the Gospel. Papias tells us that Matthew collected the sayings of Jesus in the Hebrew tongue. First from hurried scraps and notes, then parables and teachings, and finally discourse, sermons and prayers the words of Jesus were kept alive for future believers. Since Mark had recorded the events of Jesus' ministry, Matthew could concentrate on the sayings. Now imagine the task of writing the complete story on a 36 foot papyrus scroll. It would be like trying to write a 22 page report on only ten sheets of post-it pages. Matthew chose the material he considered important to a Hebrew community. It was written by a Jew to convince Jews."

"A major characteristic of Matthew is to demonstrate

how often Jesus fulfilled the prophecies of the Old testament, with the obvious conclusion that he must be, therefore, the Messiah. The phrase, 'This was to fulfill what the Lord had spoken by the prophet,' appears at least 16 times. Jesus' birth and his name are the fulfillment of prophecy. The flight into Egypt, the slaughter of the children, Joseph's settlement in Nazareth, and Jesus' upbringing are all prophesied. Jesus' use of parables and his triumphal entry into Jerusalem and the betrayal for thirty pieces of silver; the casting of lots for his garments as he hung on a cross are each a fulfillment of prophecies. It is Matthew's primary purpose to show how Jesus was undeniably the Messiah."

"Matthew has a clear bias for the Jewish community. When Jesus speaks with the Syro-Phoenician woman, he states, 'I was sent only to the lost sheep of the house of Israel." (15:24). When the first evangelist were sent out, Jesus instructed them, "Go nowhere among the Gentiles, and enter no town of the Samaritans, but go rather to the lost sheep of the house of Israel' (10:5-6). Matthew does not completely exclude the Gentiles. 'Many are to come from the east and the west to sit down in the kingdom of God.' (8:11) The gospel is to be preached to the entire world (24:14). And it is Matthew who gives us the great marching orders, 'Go, therefore, and make disciples of all nations' (28:19). This gospel is first interested in the Jews, but it foresees the day when all nations will be gathered in."

"This Jewish bias is also seen in Matthew's attitude to the Law. Jesus came not to destroy, but to fulfill the Law; and again, the least part of the Law will not pass away. 'The righteousness of the Christian must exceed the righteousness of the scribes and Pharisees.' (5:17-20) Matthew was written by one who knew and loved the Law, and who saw that even the Law has its place in the Christian life."

" This brings up an apparent paradox. The scribes and Pharisees are given a very special authority. But at the same time there is no gospel which so sternly and consistently condemns them. At the very beginning, John the Baptist has a savage denunciation of them as a "brood of vipers" (3:7-12). They complain that Jesus eats with tax-collectors and sinners (9:11). They ascribe the power of Jesus, not to God, but to the prince of devils (12:24). They plot to destroy him (12:14). The disciples are warned against the evil teaching of the scribes and Pharisees (16:12). They are like evil plants, doomed to be rooted out (15:13). They are quite unable to read the signs of the times (16:3). They are the murderers of the prophets (21:41). There is nothing that compares with chapter 23, which is a condemnation, not of what the Pharisees teach, but what they are. Matthew condemns them for falling so far short of their own teaching, and far below the ideal of what they ought to be."

"Another characteristic of Matthew is his special interest in the Church. In fact, he is the only gospel writer who uses the word "church" at all. Only Matthew introduces the passage about the Church after Peter's confession at Caesarea Philippi. Only Matthew says that disputes are to be settled by the Church (18:17). By the time the Gospel of Matthew came to be written, the Church had become a reality, organized as a dominant factor in the life of the Christians."

"Matthew has a strong interest in the apocalypse, all that Jesus said about his own second coming, about the end of the world and the coming judgment (chapter 24). Matthew alone has the parables of the talents (25:14-30), the wise and foolish virgins (25:1-13), and the sheep and the goats (25:31-46)."

"However, Matthew's strongest characteristic is his emphasis as a teaching gospel. His ability to gather and systematize the lessons of Jesus is produced in five great blocks on the Kingdom of God. They are:

1.) The Sermon on the Mount (chapters 5-7);
2.) The duties of the leaders of the kingdom (chapter 10);
3.) The parables of the kingdom (chapter 13);
4.) The greatness and forgiveness in the kingdom (chapter 18);
5.) The coming of the King (chapters 24, 25)."

"Matthew has one final characteristic; his dominant idea that of Jesus as King! He writes to demonstrate the royalty of Jesus. The genealogy at the first of the book is to prove that Jesus is the Son of David, which is a title and a Messianic claim. Matthew uses that title more than any other writer, three times. The wise men come looking for him who is born King of the Jews (2:2). In the Sermon on the Mount, Matthew shows us Jesus, quoting the law, and five times abrogating it with a regal, 'But I say to you...' The triumphal entry into Jerusalem is a deliberate dramatized claim to be King (21:1-11). At his trial before Pilate, Jesus deliberately accepts the name of King (27:11); on the cross that became the instrument of his death, the title of King of the Jews was affixed, even in mockery (27:37). The final claim of Jesus is, 'All authority...has been given to me (28:18).'"

"Matthew's picture of Jesus is of a man born to be King!

Jesus walks through his pages as if in the purple and gold robe of royalty."

Mike had been listening so carefully, he nearly flinched when he understood that Fr. Lopez was finished. Without giving a thought to protocol, Mike applauded. A smattering around him joined, then stopped. Mike continued to clap his hands, until the whole class was joined in.

Fr. Lopez's smile grew even brighter. He waved his hand saying, "Thank you, Mr. O'Malley, and class. I will take that as a sound 'Amen!'"

Mike's Notebook: *Keep in mind that what makes a task unpleasant is your attitude toward it. Acknowledge your resistance, quickly let it go, and many of the things you once dreaded will become no problem at all"*

*How do I feel about that? I have a distinct advantage over those who do not get it!.*

Dr. Crumb Notebook: *Tennessee Williams makes the point that when you are constantly on the lookout for limitations, you invite those limitations into your life. Choose instead to allow more of the goodness and wholeness that makes life so beautiful and miraculous. Keep your focus on the positive possibilities, and put your energy into bringing those possibilities to life. When you are busy with creative accomplishment, fewer troubles will be able to find you.*

*How do I feel about this? There are big secrets to having a big life. This is one of them!*

Mike realized that only five weeks into the new study year, he was lagging behind in his reading. He dedicated the weekend entirely to study and made a new friend.

"Patrick of Ireland 390? – 461?: Ireland's patron saint was born somewhere on the west coast of England or Scotland, accounts of the place and date are vague and differ widely. At the age of sixteen he was captured by Irish pirates and kept as a slave for six years. While he tended his master's herd, he learned to pray. "In a single day," he tells in his autobiography, "I said so many as a hundred prayers.... I used to stay in the woods and on the mountain, and before the dawn I would be roused to prayer, in snow and frost and rain.... Because then the spirit was fervent within."

"Eventually he escaped, found his family again and trained for the priesthood. He was sent as a missionary to Ireland by the pope, and set up a bishopric at Armagh. From here he travelled all over the country founding churches and monasteries. He was very conscious of his lack of learning and eager to promote education."

"Many legends have grown up around him, but it is certainly true that Patrick was the major influence in converting Ireland to the Christian faith. His writings are the earliest British Christian literature. One of his prayers lives on even though it has been modified from Patrick's original version called the Breastplate: 'I bind unto myself today the power of God to hold and lead, His eye to watch, his might to stay, his ear to hearken to my need. The wisdom of my God to teach, his hand to guide, his shield to ward; the word of God to give me speech, his heavenly host to be my guard.'

'Christ be with me, Christ within me, Christ behind me, Christ before me, Christ beside me, Christ to win me, Christ to comfort and restore me, Christ beneath me Christ above me, Christ in quiet, Christ in danger, Christ in mouth of friend or stranger.'"

"'Bind unto myself the name, the strong name of the

Trinity; by invocation of the same, the Three in One, the One in Three, of whom all nature hath creation; Eternal Father, Spirit, Word, praise to the Lord of my salvation, Salvation is of the Lord."

Note for further discussion: The Celtic Prayers come from these first Christians outside the Roman Empire. In the fifth century they were cut off from the rest of the church by the barbarian invasions. They developed their own distinctive forms of life and worship. Not until the eleventh century were they again integrated with the rest of the church. Their prayer literature, like that of other Celtic languages, arose as the entertainment of an aristocratic social system. It was composed by paid writers supported by the court.

Dr Crumb Notebook: *"Take the time and do the work to fully know what you truly desire. The more clearly you know what that is, the more surely you can make it real."*

*How do I feel about that? Reality is not a condition of creation but rather a quality of experience.*

The main building doors were locked at 9:00 p.m. It was an easy task that Mike enjoyed. It marked the end of another day, and the beginning of another night of study. One rainy evening he was almost finished when a voice called for his attention from the parlor just off the main entrance of the women's dorm, "Mike it's a cold evening. Would you like a cup of tea?" He recognized Caroline from his Economics class.

He slowed, but kept moving toward the back door. "Sorry, there's no drinking allowed on duty." His smile and voice were warm to her.

"Not even a warm cup to chase away the chill?" she tried again.

"Sorry," he said turning the corner. "I'm on the clock." As he left he wondered how often he had received such a pleasant invitation, and how easily he had allowed it to pass. Perhaps this was an example of "squander," that Dr. Joneses had pointed to when he said we often let pass by a vast number of small opportunities as we look for the one big opportunity.

Dr Crumb Notebook: *"The world you see is a reflection of what you think. The values by which you live are constantly coming back to you. Your life embodies those ideas to which you give your complete and persistent attention. A life sincerely focused upon peace and happiness is a life filled with peace and happiness."*

*How do I feel about that? This is a warning that I get to choose my own destiny!*

Church History Notebook: Father Winslow said, "Let's meet one of the most enlightened men of the eleventh century, St. Anselm. I like what he said about education, for example. 'If you planted a tree in your garden, and bound it on all sides, so that it could not spread out its branches, what kind of tree would it prove to be when after several years you gave it room, at last, to spread? Would it not be useless with its branches all twisted and tangled? But that is how you treat your boys!' Anselm expressed those broad human sympathies in a variety of actions, from campaigning against the human slave trade, to rebuking a boy for tying a bird's legs together."

"The son of a spendthrift Lombard nobleman, Anselm left home after a quarrel with his father. He went to study under Lanfranc at Bec in Normandy, where he specialized in the study of Augustine and wrote important theological works. He went on to succeed Lanfranc in two positions – first as Abbot of Bec, and then as Archbishop of Canterbury. Despite being exiled twice by King William Rufus, he was reconciled to the king and died in office at nearly eighty. Perhaps his most familiar prayer is the Desire For God: 'O Lord our God, grant us grace to desire you with our whole heart, that so desiring we may seek and find you, and so finding you, may love you, and loving you, may hate those sins from which you have redeemed us.'"

Lent ushered in the season of preparation for Easter, and the deadline for midterms and major papers. To call it easy would be an untruth; it was very challenging. But it was doable, and Mike was committed. When the grades were posted he was more than satisfied. His name was in the top ten percent of freshmen! He received a note from Fr. James, the Registrar, giving him praise and continued encouragement. He was proving the validity of their special plan.

Econ Notebook: *"Make your image of yourself and your life a positive one, and you will program yourself for real, sustained success. Imagine yourself at your very best, and hold that image firmly in your mind, day after day, moment by moment. What you are able to imagine, you are able to create and experience. Dare to imagine, then put your precious time to good use by bringing your imagination to life."*

*How do I feel about that? A big God has big plans; it's my chore to imagine them.*

Fr. Lopez was more animated than usual; he clapped his hands for the class's attention, and announced: "Take a deep breath for we are about to dive into my favorite and perhaps the most challenging Gospel, that of Luke, the universal Gospel. The theologian James Denny was once asked if he could recommend a good book of the life of Jesus. After only a moment's thought he answered, 'Have you tried the one Luke wrote?'"

"Luke was a Gentile; and he holds the distinguished honor of penning the majority of the New Testament. He was a physician (Col.4:14), and the travelling companion of Paul; he is compiling a record of events conveyed to him by eye-witnesses, for he himself is not one. The book was addressed to a man called Theophilus. He is called "most excellent," a title usually used for high officials in the Roman government. It could also be the term used for a person who is a lover (philein) of God (Theos), a book used to tell the whole story to an earnest inquirer. The Church has given him the emblem of the calf, a sacrifice for the entire world. Luke broke down the barriers between Jew and Gentile, saint and sinner, slave and free alike. He shows us a picture of the Savior of the world. Keep that in mind as we set down the characteristics of this gospel."

"First and foremost, Luke's gospel is an exceedingly careful work. The Greek is notably good, probably the best we can find in the New Testament. He attempts to affix the date with no less than six well known officials, trying to be as accurate as possible. It is clear that Luke wrote mainly for a Gentile audience, by using a Roman emperor, and a Roman governor, before mentioning the Hebrew tetrarchs and high priest. He does not mention the fulfillment of Old Testament prophecies. He usually gives the Greek equivalent for Hebrew words so that a Greek reader would be able to understand. Simon the Cananaean becomes Simon the Zealot. Golgotha is called Kranion; both names mean "place of the skull." Luke never uses the Hebrew term, "Rabbi," but the Greek, "Master." Finally, Luke traces the genealogy of Jesus not to David, as does Matthew, but to Adam, the first of the human race. Perhaps it is because of this first characteristic that we find Luke the easiest to read; it is written for people like us!"

"Luke's Gospel is specially the gospel of prayer. At all the great moments of his life, Jesus is shown in an attitude of prayer. He prayed before his baptism; before the first encounter with the Pharisees (5:16); before he chose his inner twelve disciples (6:12); before he asked them who they considered him to be; before his first prediction of his own death (9:18); at the transfiguration (9:29); on the Mount of Olives (22:42); and upon the cross (23:46). Only Luke tells us that Jesus prayed for Peter in his hour of testing (22:32). Only Luke has the disciples asking Jesus to teach them to pray (11:1,) leading to the universal "Lord's Prayer," without the later addition of a benediction contained in Matthew (6:13). He alone shows us the parables of the two men who went into the temple to pray, known as the "Sinner's Prayer," or the friend at midnight (11:5-13) and the unjust judge (18:1-8). To Luke the open door of prayer was one of the most precious treasures in the world."

"Here is also a Gospel for women. In the Jewish Morning Prayer, a man thanked God that he had not made him a 'Gentile, a slave, or a woman.' But Luke gives a very special place to women. The birth narrative is told from Mary's point of view. It is in Luke that we read of Elizabeth, of Anna, of the widow of Nain, of the woman who anointed Jesus' feet in the home of Simon the Pharisee. It is Luke who makes vivid the pictures of Mary and Martha, and of Mary Magdalene. In the region of Macedonia, women enjoyed a more emancipated status, which may be another clue in Luke's identity."

"In Luke, the phrase, "praising God" occurs more often

than in all the rest of the New Testament put together. This praise reaches its peak in three great hymns the Church has sung through the generations: the Magnificat (1:46-55), the Benedictus (1:68-79) and the Nunc Dimittis (2:29-32.) There is radiance in Luke's gospel which is announced with angelic anthem, and echoed by glorifying shepherds, as if the sheen of heaven has touched the things of earth."

"But the outstanding characteristic of Luke is that it is the universal gospel. All barriers are down; Jesus Christ is for all people without distinction.

The kingdom of heaven is not shut to the Samaritans (9:51-6). Luke alone tells the parable of the Good Samaritan (10:30-7). The one grateful leper is a Samaritan (17:11-19.) Luke refuses to shut the door on anyone.

Luke shows Jesus speaking with approval of a Gentile, whom an orthodox Jew would have considered unclean: he shows us citing the widow of Zarephath and Naaman the Syrian as shining examples (4:25-7.) The Roman Centurion is praised for the greatness of his faith (7:9), and Luke tells us of the words of Jesus, "People will come from east and west, from north and south, and will eat in the kingdom of God" (13:29).

Luke is supremely interested in the poor. When Mary brings her offering for her purification it is identified as the offering of the poor (2:24.) When the disciples of John come to Jesus asking, "Are you the One, or should we look for another?" Jesus' answer concludes "...and the poor have good news brought to them," (17:22). Luke alone tells us the parable of the rich man and Lazarus; the poor man (16:19-31). In Luke's account of the beatitudes he records Jesus' words,

"Blessed are you poor" (6:20) rather than Matthew's, 'Blessed are the poor in spirit,' Luke's gospel has been called the 'gospel of the underdog'. His heart reaches out to everyone for whom life is an unequal struggle."

The obvious conclusion, therefore, is Luke's portrayal of Jesus as a friend of outcasts and sinners. He alone tells of the woman who anointed the feet of Jesus, bathing them with her tears and wiping them with her hair (7:36-50); of Zachaeus, the tree-climbing tax collector (19:1-10); of the penitent thief (23:43); and he alone has the immortal story of the prodigal son and the loving father (15:11-32.) Luke omits the admonition given the first evangelistic team to avoid Samaria or Gentiles. All four gospels quote Isaiah 40 when they give the message of John the Baptist, 'Prepare the way of the Lord…;' but only Luke continues the quote to its triumphant conclusion, 'And all flesh shall see the salvation of God' (Isaiah 40:3-5; Luke 3:4,6). Luke of all the gospel writers sees no limits to the love of God."

"I do believe that of all the gospel writers, the one I would most like to meet is Luke the Macedonian physician with the tremendous vision of the infinite sweep of the love of God. To call him outstanding would have been a pale understatement." Fr. Lopez closed his notes with a satisfied smile. The silence that held the room was evidence of the listener's attention. Then Mike began to applaud, again.

Notebook: *Fr Joneses was on a roll:"Does it seem to you that all the best opportunities have already been claimed? Actually nothing could be further from the truth. There are more valuable opportunities available to you today than there ever have been before. And the best part is that they grow more numerous with each passing moment. Each opportunity that is followed and fulfilled gives birth to even more opportunities. Not only are the best opportunities not running out, they are growing in number and value!"*

*How do I feel about that? It makes me eager to be alive tomorrow! I am not escaping today, but claiming a bold, powerful, thrilling new day.*

Fr. Winslow seemed almost relieved when he said, "The final saint to come to our attention as this quarter comes to an end, is the one everyone agrees must be canonized, Francis of Assisi. When we first meet him we may not see his saintliness, but isn't that the beauty of God's handiwork? Born in 1181, the son of a wealthy cloth merchant, he looked nothing like a spiritual leader. In a war between Assisi and Perugia, Francis was taken prisoner and became seriously ill. When he was released he made a pilgrimage to Rome, then returned to his home, a changing man. He had found the peacefulness of prayer. One day while praying in the ruined church of San Damiano, he clearly heard a voice saying, 'Go, and repair my house.' Taking the words literally, he sold some of his father's cloth and offered the money to the priest to rebuild the church."

"Would you believe it if I told you this caused some conflict with his family? It came to a crisis when Francis stripped off all his clothes in the marketplace and returned them to his father. From that moment, he considered himself 'married to Lady Poverty.'"

"With clothes given by the bishop, and money he had begged, Francis went off to rebuild San Damiano. He was soon joined by seven disciples, the first of what was to become the vast order of Franciscan friars. They lived in extreme poverty, preaching, laboring and serving the needy."

"Many stories, true and legendary, have grown up around Francis: his preaching to the birds, his taming of a wolf, his receiving the stigmata, the wounds of Jesus. One of his more ambitious, if less successful, ventures was an effort to convert the Saracens. At age forty-five, his life ended in poverty." Tears were shed from an emotional priest.

History Notebook: *"The victories bring joy and new opportunities. The defeats bring wisdom, strength, determination, and new opportunities. In this way life moves continually forward. In each moment, you can build on whatever has come before."*

*How do I feel about that? I have been under-appreciating my home and past. There were rich lessons to learn there that I overlooked, and did not appreciate.*

Econ Notebook: *"Responsibility can be difficult, time-consuming, unfair, inconvenient, and uncomfortable. Yet it also brings you to a level of empowerment that cannot be reached in any other way. At the heart of true achievement is responsibility. An essential element of meaningful fulfillment is responsibility. Every great opportunity is an opportunity to take responsibility. Whatever the situation, the successful way forward is to act with responsibility."*

*How do I feel about that? The reoccurring theme I have discovered is "I have a choice," and this is especially true. Honesty is no accident.*

Fr. Lopez was seated when the class entered. He asked their permission to attempt a major presentation of their fourth part of the synoptic problem, and warned them that they may run a bit late. "For many Christians, the Gospel according to John is the most precious book in the New Testament. It is the book on which above all they feed their minds and nourish their hearts, and in which they rest their souls. Ask yourself what was the very first piece of scripture you memorized; for most of us it was, 'For God so loved the world...' (3:16) Very often in stained glass windows and church art, John is symbolized by an eagle, for he has a penetrating gaze into the eternal mysteries, the eternal truths, perhaps the very mind of God. Many people find themselves closer to God and to Jesus when reading this gospel than any other book in the world."

"But we only have to read this fourth gospel in the most cursory way to see that it is quite different from the other three. It, for example, omits a birth narrative, or an account of the baptism of Jesus, and doesn't mention the temptations; it tells nothing of the Last Supper, nothing of Gethsemane, and nothing of the ascension. It has no word of the healing of people possessed by devils or evil spirits. Perhaps most surprising, it has no parable stories, which are such a priceless part of the other three gospels. In those other three, Jesus speaks in these memorable stories, or in short vivid sentences which stick in the memory. Here in John's Gospel, the speeches of Jesus are often a whole chapter long and are involved, argumentative pronouncements quite unlike the unforgettable style of the other three."

"More surprising, the account of the fourth gospel in portraying the facts and ministry of the life of Jesus are often different from that of the other three.

a). John has a different account of the *beginning of the ministry of Jesus*. In the other three it is quite clear that Jesus did not emerge as a preacher until after John the Baptist had been imprisoned. In the fourth gospel, however, there is a considerable period during which the ministry of Jesus overlapped with the activity of John the Baptist (3:22-30; 4:1-2).

b). John has a different account of the *scene of Jesus' ministry*.

In the three gospels, the main scene is Galilee or the road to Jerusalem. Jesus is in the great city only during the final week of his life. In the forth gospel, the main scene is Jerusalem and Judea, with only occasional withdrawals to Galilee. In fact, after the Feast of Dedication, which is in wintertime, he never leaves Jerusalem. That would be a stay of several months from winter to springtime and the Passover when he was crucified.

"It was this difference of scene which provided an early church historian, Eusebius, with an explanation of the difference between the fourth gospel and the other three. He said that many people in his day (about AD 300) believed that the evangelism trail called Matthew after he had written his account of the sayings of Jesus. Mark and Luke were also on the mission road with their church building, while John was still preaching the story of Jesus. He bore witness to the accuracy of their works, 'but there was lacking in them an account of the deeds done by Christ at the beginning of his ministry...' which is what John has offered to us. There is no contradiction."

"John has a different account of the duration of Jesus' ministry. The other writers imply that it only lasted one year, because there is only one reference in each account of a Passover Feast. In John, there are three Passovers, one at the cleansing of the temple (2:13); one near the feeding of the 5000 (6:4); and the final Passover when Jesus went to the cross. Three years was scarce enough time for all that was said and done by Jesus to reveal a new way of seeing God, and a new covenant with him."

"It sometimes happens that John differs in matter of fact with the other three. There are two examples: John puts the cleansing of the temple at the beginning of Jesus ministry

(2:13) the others put it at the end. Second, John dates the crucifixion of Jesus on the day before Passover, while the others date it on the day of the Passover."

"One thing is certain. If John differs from the others it is not because of ignorance or lack of information. He gives us much information that the others don't mention. John alone tells of the wedding feast at Cana of Galilee (2:1-11); of the night conversation with Nicodemus (3:1-15); of the woman of Samaria (4); of the raising of Lazarus (11); of the way in which Jesus washed the disciples' feet (13:1-17); of Jesus' wonderful teaching about the Holy Spirit, the Comforter, which is scattered through chapters 14 – 17. It is only in John that Thomas speaks; that Andrew becomes a real personality, that we get a glimpse of the character of Philip, that we hear the carping protest of Judas at the anointing in Bethany; and the strange thing is that these little extra touches are very revealing, which etch each one in an unforgettable way."

"Again and again John has little extra details which read like the memories of someone who was there. The loaves that the boy brought to Jesus were *barley loaves;* when Jesus came to the disciples as they were crossing the lake in the storm, they had rowed about *three or four miles*; there were *six stone water pots* at Cana of Galilee. It is only John who tells of the *four soldiers gambling* for the seamless outer robe as Jesus dies; he knows the exact weight of the *myrrh and alo*es which were used to anoint the body of Jesus; and he remembers how the *fragrance of the perfume* ointment filled the house in Bethany. Many of these apparently unimportant details add color and reality to the story of Jesus' ministry."

"Let's try to focus on the purpose of John's Gospel. What

was his aim in writing it? We believe it was written in the last decade of the first century. By that time two special features had emerged in the situation of the Christian Church. First, Christianity had gone out into the Gentile world, which is to say it was no longer predominantly Hebrew. It therefore had to be restated in different categories and terms of the Greek world. Secondly, there was the rise of heresy. Both of these new factors are addressed in this fourth gospel."

"Greeks were among the world's greatest thinkers. Was it necessary for them to abandon their entire great intellectual heritage in order to think in Jewish terms and categories of thought? John realized there were two great conceptions:"

"They had the concept of the *Logos,* which in Greek means two things – it means word, and it means reason. Jews were entirely familiar with the all-powerful word of God. "God said, 'Let there be light' and there was light." The Greeks also were familiar with the thought of reason, for when they observed the world around them, the seasons, the stars with their unfaltering paths, nature had laws. What produced that order? Greeks answered unhesitatingly: "The Logos, the mind of God!" They went on to say, "What gives human beings power to think, to reason, to know?" and they unhesitatingly came to the same conclusion, the Logos, the mind of God dwelling within an individual makes that person a thinking rational being. John seized on this. It was in this way that he thought of Jesus. "In the beginning was the Logos," (1:1). He had found a fresh way to speak of Jesus, a category in which Jesus was presented as nothing less than God acting in human form."

"The Greeks had the concept of *two worlds.* One was the world in which we live, a wonderful world in its way, but one of shadows, copies and unrealities. The other was the real world, in which great realities and absolutes stand forever. To the Greeks, the unseen world was the real one; the seen world only a copy, a shadowy unreality. The great problem was how to get into this world of reality from our partial and limited one, how to get out of our shadows into the eternal truth."

"John declares that is exactly what Jesus enables us to do. He is reality come to earth. The Greek word for real is *alethinos*. So John explains that Jesus is the *real* light, (1:9) the *real* bread, (6:32) Jesus is the *real* vine; (15:1) to Jesus belongs the *real* judgment (8:16). Jesus alone has reality in our worlds of shadow and imperfections. And from that, this important insight follows: Every action that Jesus did was not only an act in time, but a window which allows us to see into eternity. That's what John means when he talks of Jesus' miracles as *signs*. The wonderful works of Jesus were not simply wonderful; they were windows opening to the reality which is God. (Let's talk later about how this causes John to deal differently with the miracles stories than the other three gospel writers.)"

"The second part of John's purpose was to correct the rise of heresies in the growing Church. Theologies and creeds were being formulated and stated; and inevitably the thought of some people went down mistaken ways, and heresies resulted. A heresy is seldom a complete untruth; it usually results when one part of the truth is unduly emphasized."

"There were certain Jewish Christians who gave John the Baptist too much status. He walked in the prophetic succession, and spoke with the authority of significance. We know that he had disciples, who came to Jesus questioning his identity (Matt 11:3). In later times there was an accepted sect of John the

Baptist within the Jewish faith. In Acts 19:1-7 we come upon a little group of twelve on the fringe of the Christian Church who had never moved beyond the baptism of John. Over and over the fourth gospel quietly, but definitely relegates John to his proper place. Over and over again, John himself denies that he has ever claimed or possessed the highest place, and without qualifications yields to Jesus."

"Of greater significance to the growing Church was the heresy called by the general name of *Gnosticism*. Without some understanding of it, much of John's greatness and much of his purpose will be missed. The basic doctrine of the Gnostics was that matter is essentially evil, and spirit is essentially good. The Gnostics went on to argue that on that basis God himself cannot touch matter, and therefore could not have had anything to do with the world's creation. That is why John begins his Gospel with the ringing statement 'All things were created by him and without him not one thing came into being.' (1:3) That is why John insists that, 'God so loved the world,' (3:16) In the face of Gnostics who so mistakenly spiritualized God into a being who could not possibly have anything to do with the world, John presents the Christian doctrine of the God who made the world and whose presence fills the world he has made."

"On one hand, there is no gospel which so uncompromisingly stresses the real humanity of Jesus. He was angry with those who bought and sold in the Temple courts (2:15); he was physically tired as he sat by the well which was near Sychar in Samaria (4:6); his disciples offered him food in the way they would offer it to a hungry man (4:31); he had sympathy for those who were hungry, and those who were afraid (6:5,20);

he knew grief and wept the tears that any mourner might (11:33); and in the agony of the cross the cry of his parched lips was, 'I thirst.' (19:28) It is truly a human Jesus that the fourth gospel reveals."

"On the other hand there is no gospel which sets before us such a view of the deity of Jesus. He was in the beginning with God (1:2). 'Before Abraham was, I am,' said Jesus (8:58). Again and again he speaks of his coming down from heaven (6:33ff) But he also had a fore-knowledge that in John's view was miraculous. Jesus knew the past record of the woman of Samaria (4:16); apparently without anyone telling him, he knew how long the man beside the healing pool had been sick; (5:6) before he asked it, he knew the answer to the question put to Philip (6:6) he knew that Judas would betray him (6:61). To counter the Gnostics and their strange beliefs, John presents us with a Jesus who is undeniably human and yet was undeniably divine."

"Who is this disciple, the only one of Jesus' chosen twelve to die of natural causes? He was the younger son of Zebedee, a fisherman on the Sea of Galilee who was sufficiently well off to hire servants to help him (Mark 1:19). John's mother was Salome, and it seems likely that she was the sister of Mary, the mother of Jesus (Mark 16:1). We know him as one of the leaders of the twelve; he was one of the inner circle of Jesus' closest friends; and at the same time he was a man of temper, ambition, and intolerance, yet one of great courage. It is the great biblical scholar Jerome who tells the story of the last words of John. When he was dying, his friends asked if he had any last message to leave them. 'Little children,' he said, 'love one another.' Again and again he repeated it; and they asked him if that was all he had to say. "It is enough," he said, "for it is the Lord's command.' That tells us of the man, a figure of fiery temper, of wide ambition, of undoubted courage, and, in the end, of gentle love. In Ephesus there were three graves of distinction, one of Mary, mother of Jesus, one of John the Apostle, and one of John, the "Elder," who was Bishop of Hierapolis, and whose dates are from about AD 70 to about AD 145".

"A. H. N. Green Armytage wrote in his book, *John, Who Saw*, 'Mark suits the *missionary* with his clear-cut account of the facts of Jesus' life; Matthew suits the *teacher* with his systematic account of the teaching of Jesus; Luke suits the *parish minister or priest* with his wide sympathy and his picture of Jesus as a friend of all; but in John is the gospel of the *contemplative*."

"Our final observation introduces a strange thing. In the fourth gospel, John is never mentioned by name. The "beloved disciple" is referenced at the Last Supper, next to Jesus, at the cross receiving the care of Jesus' mother, with Peter when Mary Magdalene returned from the tomb that first Easter morning, and he was present at the last resurrection appearance of Jesus by the lakeside. Then too, the fourth gospel has a person we might call the "witness." When Jesus receives that final spear-thrust upon the cross, there follows this comment, 'He who saw this has testified so that you might believe. His testimony is true, and he knows he tells the truth.' (19:35). At the end of the gospel comes the statement that it was the beloved disciple who testified of these things, 'and we know that his testimony is true,' (21:24)".

"The more we know about the Fourth Gospel, the more precious it becomes. For seventy years, John had thought of

Jesus. Day by day, the Holy Spirit had opened out to him the meaning of what Jesus said. So when John was near his last days, he and his friends sat down to remember. John the elder held the pen to write for his mentor and teacher, John the Apostle; and the last of the apostles set down not only what he had heard Jesus say, but also what he now knew Jesus had meant. He remembered how Jesus had said, 'I still have many things to say to you, but you cannot bear them now. When the Spirit of truth comes, he will guide you into all the truth.' (16:12)."

"There were many things which he had not understood seventy years ago; there were many things which in those seventy years the Spirit of truth had revealed to him. These things John set down even as the eternal glory was dawning upon him. When we read this gospel, let us remember that we are reading the gospel which of all the gospels is most the work of the Holy Spirit, speaking to us of the things which Jesus meant, speaking through the mind and memory of John the apostle and by the pen of John the elder. Behind this gospel is the whole church at Ephesus, the whole company of the saints, the last of the apostles, the Holy Spirit and the Risen Christ himself."

Fr. Lopez closed his notebook firmly, gave a sigh, and said, "If you recall just a part of all that, you will breeze through the final exam. I am proud of your endurance."

Yet again, Mike began an applause that was more energetically joined by the rest of the class.

Econ Notebook: *"If you are not moving forward, it is because you are holding yourself back. You may have chosen to blame your lack of progress on outside factors, yet deep down you know that you are the primary factor. It doesn't really matter why or how you have chosen to prevent yourself from achieving your desired results. What is crucial is that you simply get out of the way and allow yourself to move forward."*

How do I feel about that? It is easier to blame, to become a victim, than to accept success.

As Mike was leaving the Literature class, he was looking forward to a few hours of sleep before his security duties. A happy lady skipped up to him asking if she could have a minute of his time. Looking at her brown hair and deep brown eyes, he was happy to oblige her.

"Mike, I am Gloria Gilles; I'm sorry to say that I know of you, but we haven't met. I'm not going to let that stop me from asking a question, however. Would you consider attending the Sadie Hawkins Dance with me on April 1st? If you have jeans and a flannel shirt, I'll get matching neckerchiefs and we'll be all set." Her eager expression was very difficult to deny.

"Wow, that's a generous offer, Gloria. By the way, it is a pleasure to meet you. You know, however, that I have the security job that keeps me from saying 'yes, indeed.'"

She placed her hand on his armful of books. "Could you go to work a little late?" He was struck by her positive attempt to solve his dilemma.

"You know," he said apologetically, "I need to lock up at 9:00 o'clock. It's my job."

"Well, maybe you could just be here for the..." A nervous blush turned her neck rosy. "I'll tell you the truth, I would very much enjoy your company, but there is another reason I'm inviting you. The past two dances have been targeted by guys from Portland State. They think it's funny to crash our party. I know your reputation as a no-nonsense security, and thought it might level the field." She shook her head.

"That is the sweetest invitation I have ever had," he replied with a grin. "And I think I can plan to lock up at 9:00 and spend the rest of the evening keeping things under control. But I have to warn you I'm a much better wrestler than a dancer." They shared a happy chuckle.

"My dad used to say that he was a terrible dancer, so he just held mom while she did the footwork. Let's eat in the cafeteria, then trip the light fantastic. Is that a deal?"

He held out his hand for a friendly shake, and noticed her glance at his hearing aid. "Yeah, they are my souvenirs from Korea," he said softly.

"I'm sorry; I didn't mean to stare. A war seems a world away until you see the results of it." Her hand continued to hold his. "I've never known a warrior."

He released his hand from hers, saying, "It was a world away, and although it has been almost a year, I can still smell the ugliness of battle even if I can't hear it." Then turning toward the door, he said, "I'll see you for supper on April Fool's Day, O.K.?"

"You wouldn't play a prank on a girl now, would you?" The question was asked with a twinkle in her eye, and Mike knew she was an extraordinary lady.

The two weeks slowly passed with classes, study, rest, security, study, classes again. He did have time to purchase a red flannel shirt that seemed just right. When they met in the cafeteria, her wide smile assured him it was the perfect plaid; it matched her's. A very ordinary but memorable supper was followed by a short walk to the student commons, where she held his arm as they stood in line to get in. After an hour and a half of chatting with her friends and trying his ability on the dance floor, he excused himself to do his lock-up duties. Fifteen minutes later he returned, with his batons. He placed them under his jacket which was under their table.

It was just after 10 o'clock when they heard loud voices coming from the front doors. Shouting and laughter was a trouble sign to Mike. He picked up his batons, fastening the lanyards on his wrists, and asked the dancers to clear the floor. As the spearhead of boisterous young men entered the commons, they were surprised to see that most people were seated, some standing around the wall, but only one figure was standing in the dance floor light. He was wearing a red plaid shirt and seemed ready to meet them.

"Hey, cowboy, where's the rodeo?" one of them asked.

Mike counted seven. "Gentlemen, may I invite you to leave quietly, before this gets out of hand?" He felt calm and focused.

"Piss off, jerk. We want to have some fun. Sit down or get hurt." They began moving toward him.

Mike said in a stronger voice, "Would someone call the switchboard for some ambulances." Then more gently, "This is a terrible plan, guys. You are almost through the quarter. Don't screw it up. You can still turn around and leave. No one has been hurt."

"Yeah dick head, but you are about to be." They were getting close. Mike dropped one foot behind himself as a brace. Then he noticed the one on the left side had a knife.

They were too bunched up for an effective assault. Mike's first strike was the wrist of the knife-holder, and he struck full-force. The target screamed as the bones broke, and the knife went sliding across the floor. No one was prepared for the on-slot of both batons. One was jammed into a soft stomach, knocking the air out of an attacker, while the other was chopping down on a collarbone. It was so fast no one could follow them. An elbow, a knee, another wrist, another elbow, were targeted and hit. Even hands were a fragile target, with bones easily broken; the battle was over for that attacker too. Witnesses would agree that Mike scarcely moved, while the seven were piled in front of him. He was careful not to hit anyone in the head, but effectively struck just about everything else. Then the only sound in the commons was whimpering.

The students were filing out when the police and ambulances arrived. The officer in charge wanted to know where the ones who had done the damage were, and could hardly believe that just one security guard had accomplished all this mayhem. Gail and several others had waited to give their account of the incident. She especially wanted to apologize to Mike for putting him in harm's way. Finally, when they had all given their statements, Mike walked four women back to their dorm.

Gail paused as the other three went inside. "Mike, I hope you are not angry with me for setting you up tonight." Her sincere eyes searched his. "I really am glad you agreed to come along with me, and not only because you kept us safe." She leaned into him, kissing him gently with soft warm lips. "Will we see each other again?"

"I look forward to it," he answered quietly. "Sweet dreams."

It was easy for him to care for his duties through the night, but difficult to study when her lips were on his mind.

The Provost's office called again, informing Mike there would be a meeting on Saturday. His attendance was required.

# THE CORRUPTION OF FATHER MIKE

Had the consequences not been so dire, he would have thought, "here we go again." But as he sat outside the office, waiting to face the Trustees again, there was a bad taste in his mouth, which he identified as anxiety

"So, Mr. O'Malley, we gather again under similar circumstances. You seem to be a magnet for trouble." The six Trustees stared at him with hard expressions. "Would you like to explain how all this came about this time?"

"Yes sir. Let me say first that I am sorry you must spend a Saturday dealing with this matter. I must make clear to you that I did not draw this trouble to myself, I was invited to the dance because students anticipated trouble from the Portland State men. Sadly, this has been a repeated assault by them, and our school has done nothing about it. My date, so to speak, warned me that it might happen again. I was concerned that we as a school have a reputation for being trampled. No one seemed to want to do anything about security, or have the ability. I was prepared."

"When the seven men came in threatening, I had cleared the others from the dance floor for their safety, and drew the pack into my range. One had a knife; he was the first to go down, then the others as they presented targets for me to strike. Once again, I restrained the use of force to simply control the situation. Then we called for police and ambulance help."

One of the Trustees asked, "Did you know that the wrist you shattered was that of their starting pitcher?"

Mike thought there might have been a tinge of pleasure in the question. "No sir, I did not know anything about them, and I only acted in self-defense. I believe he was armed with a knife."

The Provost said, "The police report and statements from witnesses say the same thing; but Mike, we have a problem here. This is the second time in just three months that you have been the center of a horrific incident, causing debilitating injuries to others. We don't know what to do with you." The look on his face was one of anguish. "Where did you learn to fight like that?"

Without hesitation, Mike answered, "It is not known as fighting, sir: it is self defense, protection of others. In Yokosuka Japan I had a police instructor who was Tsurugi Ken, a sword champion, who taught me the use of the Katana, a short sword about the same length as a baton."

"Are you telling us that you are a sword master?" Now the Provost was looking at Mike with a sense of awe, of surprise.

"No sir, I only learned basic moves and strikes that work with the baton too. May I say something, sir?" When permission was given, Mike said, "As I see it, this University has operated on dignity and a reputation of grace. That is a wonderful peaceful legacy, as long as it works. But it only takes a handful of ruffians or a few pranksters to demonstrate that this is basically a defenseless, weak institution." The startled reaction from the men caused him to quickly add, "I am not insulting or denigrating the school that I love. I am saying that like lambs, we have had no protection, no shepherd to maintain order. The two actions I have had to control is simply that. I have shown both our residents, and those who might visit us, that we have a shepherd who can't be pushed around. We now have their respect."

One of the Trustees smiled and said, "You have a way of putting a good spin on trouble. Do you know that the Greek word for shepherd is 'pastor?'"

## THE CORRUPTION OF FATHER MIKE

"Pastor, priest or security guard, we cannot as a University have any more of this," the Provost said firmly. "Mike, I am recommending that the Board of Trustees puts you on probation; with one more violent incident, you will be suspended. You may not agree with the decision, but I believe it is in keeping with our theological foundation. There are avenues of appeal if you so choose." He thanked them all for their time.

As Mike was leaving, two of the men were waiting for him in the hallway. One of them put his hand on Mike's shoulder and said confidentially, "We do not agree with the Provost, and believe you did the right thing in both cases. It is about time that someone around here has the spine to stand up to the bullies. We want you to forget about that suspension stuff. It will never happen as long as we are on the board." He gave a pat of affection and admiration.

Happily, May turned into the month of demand. Papers were due, then final exams. Mike was satisfied with his preparations, so there were no surprises when the grades were posted, and Fr. James invited Mike to stop by the Registrar's office.

"Congratulations, son," he began. "Our plan is working better than any of us hoped. Fr. Blake wants me to pass along his best wishes too. Your accomplishment is outstanding. I think I asked if you could just make a passing mark, and you have almost made the Dean's Honor list. We are so proud of your work. It goes without saying that the Gilman Scholarship will continue. Have you thought about fall subjects?"

"I have, sir. I believe Political Science, Psychology, and Greek 2 are each full year subjects. If I can fit in an Old Testament and a Western Civilization, I think I would have another full plate."

"How about first year Greek?" the registrar asked.

"I sort of hoped I could do that in this summer intensive."

"You know, don't you, that is a four hour per day, four days a week class? That is really a load," Fr James said with genuine concern.

"Yes sir." Then with a grin he added, "But I have nights to study, and three day weekends to catch up. I believe it is very doable."

"I love your confidence, Mike. One thing I'm concerned about is your personal life. How many times have you been off this campus?"

"Oh, I walk to the drug store, and I have taken the bus home a couple times. Mom is not very interested, or supportive. She's had a hard life. Dad's in prison in Kansas; he's a real disappointment to us. I'm glad to be in the presence of decent strong men who have shown me what character is all about."

"Would you like us to pray about that?"

"I would, very much."

# A New Path to Priesthood

Day by day, subject by subject, Mike flourished. It was suddenly the end of the first half of his senior year and he was invited to the Mount Angel Abby for a career retreat with his classmates. The pristine setting was perfect for the solitude of the monastic order. The grounds and gardens were inviting for a meditative stroll and for the more hardy, a hike into the Silverton Hills was a pleasant test. In the parlor of the main building wine and cheese was served along with the monks' signature Porter beer. For once Mike was glad to be twenty two. His invitation to this retreat had promised that it could bring a life-changing fresh direction to his life.

After the simple supper a group of vocalists led in singing chants and familiar hymns. Then Fr. James, acting as M.C. stood to begin the presentations: "I am overjoyed to welcome you to this career retreat," he began. "On our campus we have heard from leaders of industry who have given us visions of achievement, security, and wealth. We have listened to representatives of government outline how urgently we are needed to guide our nation into a new era of prosperity. We even had an entertainer praising the opportunities in the hospitality and travel sector of our world."

"Tonight we are honored to have two guests, Fr. Leonard Gregory from Redeemer of the Hills Parish in Denver

Colorado, and Fr. Francis Thomas from Holy Rosary Parish Los Angeles California. They will be sharing insights from their own experience that will help us understand the crisis in our local parishes. Please welcome with me these two notable priests." There was hearty applause. Mike noticed that Fr. Joneses was in the back, as was Fr. Lopez. He wondered if Fr. Winslow would show up too.

Fr. Gregory stepped to the microphone. He was tall and ruggedly handsome, with a carriage of confidence and vigor. "Gentlemen, it does my heart good to see you tonight . You represent a powerful fresh wave of leadership in a Church that desperately needs you. My daddy used to tell a story I want to share, about a plain country Judge who had an unusual sanity test. If someone brought a family member to the Judge to determine if they were sane or not, the Judge would take them outside the courtroom where there was a hose bib. A bucket was placed below it and the water turned on full force, filling the bucket, of course. The patient was then handed a dipper and told to empty the bucket. If they started dipping away, as fast as they could, the verdict was insane. If they turned off the water first, regardless of how unsteady or slow their hand, they could empty the bucket and earn the Judge's blessing."

"Something like this has been happening in our Church. For hundreds of years the Church has had the choicest scholars as priest candidates. Even with limited scientific knowledge we kept the advancement of society moving forward with a steady supply of leadership. Following World War II, we had a bounty of men who had found God's hand at work in their lives in a time of crisis, and chose to serve Him as priests, and filled our schools to the full"

"But wait, now ten years later, our country has been part of a dismal "Police Action" in Korea with no clear victory or accomplishment. No one has been liberated, no evil enemy overwhelmed, no victory march, and suddenly the Church is asking, 'where are the candidates?'. And to complicate that picture, each year there are about 500 priests who have reached an age where they can no longer serve, and another 200 who must leave because of illness and infirmity. We can't keep up with our loss, let alone fill growing communities with new priests. We are dipping as fast as we can, but we are not gaining on the deficit. Does it seem wise to you that we keep doing what we have been doing, that we follow the same losing path? I don't think so either."

"Do not misunderstand here, I am not suggesting that we alter the catechism, or modify the liturgy, or in any way change the sacraments, although our recent shift to a more common language has helped. Our Church has been, and will always be, the protector of the faith, and servant of the faithful. That being said, let me ask you when was your heart last stirred in a Church worship service? When were you inspired to rise up and fight on for your Lord, the Christ? When did you understand more fully that God was inviting you into a moment of divine power? I'm really sorry if you cannot remember just one such moment. That is why, I believe, our Church is in trouble." Mike was remembering the words of Fr. Blake before he went into battle for the first time, "And it did not fall!"

"I think back to a time when I, as a teenager, heard the message of the Risen Christ speaking to Peter beside the seashore so clearly that the disciple cried out, ' Lord you know that I love you!', and I wanted to shout that also. What is it that makes people want to shout, or serve, or commit their lives afresh? Gentlemen, I believe it is a renewal of homiletics, proclaiming the victorious name of Jesus so clearly that the Church is empowered, restored, redeemed! This is not an invitation to another reformation, but a revival of what Jesus told us to do originally:' Go and preach!' I believe homiletics is used by God to build and equip the Church for missions. Every observation I have been able to make leads me to conclude that proclamation is the essential ingredient in the Church's renewal, health and growth. It is also how new priests will be inspired."

"Win Arn, a prominent sociologist, says, 'In America the primary catalytic factor for growth in the local church is the priest.' In a healthy congregation the priest wants the church to grow and is willing to give the leadership that encourages that dynamic condition. He doesn't do all the work, but gives positive leadership."

"You might ask, 'How does the congregation really know the priest wants the church to grow?' I'm pretty sure it is not the hours he spends cloistered in his study in prayer, although that is good. It is not his golf handicap or the amount of time he gives to the Bingo party. They know because he proclaims it Sunday after Sunday from the pulpit. His messages lift up the priority of the Great Commission of Jesus Christ: 'Go therefore and make disciples of all nations…' His tone of voice and his whole personality communicate the urgency, the opportunity, and the joy of a dynamic congregation. From the pulpit, dealing compassionately yet firmly with the obstacles, the priest makes it clear that dynamic faith is normative for the followers of Christ. The congregation is thus led to identify and confront growth-inhibiting fears and objectives."

"A priest, trained in dynamic principles and insights, which are thoroughly Biblical, proclaims an exciting message that enables people to visualize themselves as individuals participating in the congregation in a new, positive way. They begin to see the community through dynamic eyes; they catch the vision of a dynamic, excited , and convinced leader who Sunday after Sunday, in dozens of different ways , shares a new way of seeing the local opportunities. '...lift up your eyes, and see how the fields are already white for harvest.'"

"It is through the preaching priest that members of the congregation are awakened to the unrealized potential of the local community of faith . They learn from scripture that the New testament Church grew with explosive contagion, in spite of terrible opposition or the availability of just a few great preachers like Peter or Paul. They grew because hundreds and hundreds of ordinary Christians shared with their friends, relatives, and neighbors the great possibility of new creation in Jesus Christ."

"Members of the congregation, most of whom greatly respect their priest, watch for subtle clues to his real priorities. As they listen, they become convinced that even they can become partners, effective channels, of the greatest miracle on planet earth! This is the miracle of the new birth. It becomes clear from the pulpit and from the priest that God's love is not a heavy dreadful burden to be borne, not another 'should' or 'ought' of legalism, but a glorious opportunity given to every believer A contagious excitement moves from priest to congregation to community. Do you suppose that sort of dynamic happens when the priest dully reads a homily that even bores him? Do you imagine that a hurriedly prepared or worn out treaties will hold anyone's attention? I have talked with Bishops from Maine to Montana, California to Connecticut who all share the same observation: effective, enthusiastic Biblical preaching is one of the long underestimated ingredients in dynamic healthy churches. People today are hungry for that sort of preaching, while the bottom has dropped out for ordinary topical homilies. Who cares about those? The demand has never been greater for excellent Biblical preaching by committed and excited priests."

"The Bishop of the Denver Archdiocese, has taken a bold step in the order of the priesthood. He has held to the traditional high standards of ordination, but he considers conduct to be an on-going process of demonstrating obedience to God's leadership. He holds that it is God's Church; God calls, trains, and equips priests for their duties. A priest who does not bear the dynamic fruit consistent with the Biblical design, or fails to hold to a code of righteousness, is moved to a smaller parish where he might be more capable. If, in two years on probation, he fails in that second effort, he is moved either into a post of administration or into secular employment. No longer is the priesthood a guaranteed cushion for under-achievers, however likeable they might be. The Bishop believes that in a hundred Sundays the Holy Spirit has ample opportunity to be revealed."

With a chuckle, Fr. Leonard said, "You may be wondering how long I have been at Redeemer of the Hills; eighteen years and it is still as fresh to me today as it was the very first time I stepped into their pulpit. We have started, in those years, five new satellite congregations on Denver's growing east suburbs.

We have mission projects in thirteen countries outside of the U.S. and our attendance and membership continues to exceed previous records. We are a dynamic congregation that continues to inspire me. The priest who stands with his people in hearing, seeing and experiencing the great realities that ultimately motivate the world for our Lord the Christ is a rare privilege. To witness God's forgiveness, healing and deliverance from defeat and death is a dynamic transformation that we get to share. It is through this channel that God continues to set his people free to go and grow."

"Thank you for opening this discussion and allowing me to participate. We'll have more to share in the morning. I believe the future for the church here in Portland is thrilling, amazing, dynamic beyond words. Thank you."

Mike began an applause that didn't end until all the students were joined in.

Fr. Francis made his way to the microphone, and after a bit of adjusting, he asked, "What do you recall about Thomas Aquinas?" There was a mixture of snickering and shrugs. "Yeah, me too," he said. He was rumpled and short, in contrast to Fr. Leonard. "I am grateful to be invited here this evening to do the second half of the presentation on dynamic preaching. Now that you have heard the 'why' of dynamic preaching, my task is to fill in the 'how.' You see, I did my dissertation on Thomas Aquinas," (Mike was surprised that he had a doctorate!) "and taught Church History at Carroll College in Helena, Montana. Just think, eleven years, and not one dynamic presentation. I remember that after writing theology papers that guided generations of church thought, Aquinas had a revelation he claimed was from God that made 'all I had written seem like so much straw.' Can you identify with that? Hours of study, miles of papers, more books than you can carry and what does it amount to ...so much straw! I was ready to leave the priesthood when the Bishop of the Archdiocese of Los Angeles offered me a challenge. He said there was a very small church that was struggling for its life. They needed a wise priest who could guide them. I thought it might be more because of my Latino background than my wisdom. I said 'yes' anyway. The congregation was made up of about three dozen elderly women who had tamale sales to try to keep the doors open. I quit trying to write straw, and found the center. Today Holy Rosary has seven thousand souls who come to mass each Sunday. We are an outreach center with pages of opportunities to encounter God's activity in a hurting East L.A., and a wounded world."

"Preaching that frees the church to grow begins with the sovereign action of God. That action is God's working through his Holy Spirit to convince the priest that there is a message that will in fact make a difference in human life now and for eternity. That's not straw, brothers! Unless the priest is convinced of the uniqueness and supreme importance of God's saving action in Jesus Christ, then preaching will be no more than snappy pep-talks or guilt-inflictive moralisms. The key to avoiding this pitfall is to begin at the center – the priest's personal relationship with God."

"This means that ultimately the prayer and devotional life of the priest must be recognized as that center out of which the message is to flow. Time for relationship with the Living Lord must have first priority in the priest's day. It is imperative that this be a large block of uninterrupted time. This is neither study time nor sermon preparation time, although ideas and messages will flow. It is relationship time. Without time, the relationship suffers."

"Scripture is read and reread. Chapter after chapter is received with an openness to God's message to the reader. Hand copying passages of special inspiration and personal meaning into a notebook preserves for later reflection that message heard from God's word. This nurturing influence helps the priest understand that biblical preaching is not a special formula of hermeneutics. It is rather a standing with people in the presence of the living God so that both are grasped by the vividness of that awesome reality. Contemporary preaching has too little vividness, which cannot be corrected by contrived dramatics. Preaching that builds up the church and frees it to grow comes from the heart center of one who has himself been liberated and built up by the Living Lord."

"Reading of scripture, for me, is followed by a time of listening prayer or meditation. Yes, it begins with a deep breath or two, and the relaxation of muscular tension, which opens the door for the Holy Spirit to give guidance to this arena of prayer."

"I like to use mental imagery, so I frequently see a stairway down out of a stuffy balcony filled with shadows." He smiled broadly as he parenthetically asked, "Do you suppose that is how I see academia? I picture myself slowly descending those stairs. The light increases as I make my way down. Finally there is a door at the bottom which I open, and step out into a lovely garden or courtyard with fresh mown grass and a fountain. There is blue sky over head and warm sunshine that represents the warmth of God's love I feel. A gentle breeze is a reminder of the Spirit that surrounds and welcomes me. There is a pathway into the garden. From some distance I see a man approaching. As he comes nearer his identity is clearly revealed. This is Jesus. Now is the time to simply be present with him. This is the time to listen, to be aware. Finally, it is time to raise the questions: 'Lord what do you want me to say?'" He paused for several seconds. "Lord, what is your word for me and for your people?" Again, this is a time for listening – really listening."

"Then for me, is a time to invite, in faith, others into the scene. It is a way to pray for colleagues, family, the sick, the congregation, leaders of our world. Biblical scenes of blessing, teaching, healing, commissioning are seen clearly as realities of the presence. During this time of meditation or listening prayer, there is openness to pictures and words of affirmation and hope from the Risen Lord."

"Sometimes during a meditation such as this I have seen the congregation bathed in light. At other times I have seen Jesus moving among the people – touching, healing, and forgiving them. I have seen him standing beside me during the preaching time. At other times I have experienced a connection being made between me and a depth of unfailing divine power and love."

"The meditation ends with prayers of praise and thanksgiving. The spoken prayer is primarily one of gratitude and acceptance. These are often words of commitment and dedication, spoken out of wonder and awe of the reality of this gift of God's grace in Christ Jesus through his Holy Spirit. There is no sermon preparation without this time. With it, sermon preparation becomes an exhilarating adventure. There is already a confidence, an assurance that something great is going to happen in the worship experience because something exhilarating has already happened in the life of the priest!"

"It is out of this experience of scripture reading, meditation, prayer, plus disciplined preparation that I have come to a very high view of preaching. Biblical preaching is the outward sharing of the inner visualization, and experience, of the Word of God, in an atmosphere of prayerful, expectant faith, guided by the Holy Spirit. Such preaching, when received in openness and faith, enables the listener and priest to experience, as present reality, the action of God described in the text. In other words, , true Biblical preaching is more than quotation of large quantities of Biblical material. Biblical preaching may occur in a wide variety of styles, with different interpretations of the same text. True Biblical preaching is the proclamation which is grasped by the reality of the Good News in such vivid awareness that the power and energy of God's action is experienced among priest and people as a present reality! The inner core of true Biblical preaching goes beyond scholarly principles and rules of hermeneutics."

"Fr. Johannes Hamel, a priest in East Germany, says that when preaching is done effectively in the name of Jesus Christ, the results are beyond comprehension.

'We are proclaiming a reality so immense that the very naming of it changes the situation of the hearer, because this is the event of all events. Where the gospel is preached, demons are robbed of their power; sins are forgiven; prisoners are freed; and the sorrowing find peace because of God's loving kindness. This and nothing less occurs with the delivery of such a message.'"

"Chancellor D. G. Miller shares the same high estimate of the potential of preaching when he writes: 'Preaching is not merely speech; it is an event. In true preaching, something happens. Priest and people are brought together by the living flame of truth, as oxygen and matter are joined in the living encounter by fire. The eternal problem of the priest is how to produce such a response.'"

"Think of that! When has your work been like fire? The priest must constantly be open to the guidance of the Living Fire, the Holy Spirit, in understanding and perceiving the mystery of the awesome potential of preaching. In a dynamic church there is an increasing sense of wonder about the power of the Gospel. Preaching is exalted, not for the sake of the preacher, or Rome, but out of gratitude for what God is doing in the lives of his people through his effective priests."

"To be sure, dynamic preaching will be graphic and vivid. Biblical stories will be powerfully related not for pleasant or educational reflection, but as channels of hope-bringing, life-changing, spirit-lifting truth! Modern congregations have little interest in antiquarian traditions. The stories are told because they announce present possibilities. Bartimaeus sees! Jairus rejoices! Matthew gets up from his desk with pen in hand!" Mike felt a jolt of electricity through his body. "Legion returns to his family! Zachaeus gives generously to the poor! Lazarus comes out of his tomb! Mary announces the resurrection! Thomas is convinced! Peter is restored! Suddenly priest and people are gripped by the reality that they are dealing not with what happened 1900 years ago, but with what is happening today! In the Church of Jesus Christ, isolation is overcome, sins forgiven, sickness healed, salvation experienced and lived! It is through dynamic preaching that St Peter's Church will know the miracle of rebirth!"

"It's time for me to close here, and for us to ponder all that has been said, so in conclusion let me say, that preaching can be a high adventure for priest and parish alike. Where this is true, the sermon will be perceived as related ultimately to the central issues of existence. Scripture becomes alive. The sacraments reflect the power and joy of the Spirit. Jesus is known as a living being, not a remote figure of the past. God is worshipped in joy and thanksgiving. There is a sense of hope and anticipation drawing us into the future. Let me ask you, would you like to be part of that picture? Is God calling to you tonight to become such a priest?"

"I know that something is happening here. God is at work, not only in one of you, but in many. He called me here to greet you in his name, and now in the power of his Spirit you are feeling a new certainty and boldness like never before. You are invited to enter this life-changing, burden-lifting, hope-bringing good news. Jesus said, 'Follow me. And they left their boats and followed him. Will you bow with me in prayer?"

"Give me, O Lord, a steadfast heart, which no unworthy affection may drag downward; give me an unconquered heart, which no tribulation can wear out; give me an upright heart, which no unworthy purpose may tempt aside. Bestow on me also, O Lord my God, understanding to know you, diligence to seek you, wisdom to find you, and a faithfulness that may finally embrace you, through Jesus Christ or Lord, Amen."

"Gentlemen, your attention has been magnificent! By the way, that was the prayer of Thomas Aquinas, and it was definitely not straw, if you are considering a call into the priesthood. God bless you, and goodnight."

After breakfast the next morning, The musicians returned

for some pleasant devotions, then Fr. James explained the presence of printed cards near each plate. "These cards are to help us identify candidates for the priesthood. I'm sure you have given it some prayerful thought during the night, perhaps for a long time before that. Now you can share that with us and we can help in the training process. We want to walk with you all the way to your ordination, and into parish service." He explained the steps both academic and ecclesiastic for candidacy.

Mikes heart trembled as he put his pen on the line. It would be a three year process, in which he could choose a different path if this was not for him. Did he really imagine God would use him as a priest to build the church? "Yes!" He signed the card and returned it to Fr, James, who said quietly, "I hoped you would."

Back at school he studied for a while, worked out at the gym, then sent Christmas cards to Sergeant White, Fr. Blake, and Ernie. His scribbled message in each card was: 'I have good news of great joy! Merry Christmas!'

# A Different Call

On the 16th of December, the phone in the security office rang at a quarter to ten; it was Ernie. His voice was hushed and he seemed very agitated. "I didn't think I would ever hear from you again," he began. "I desperately need your help, pal. I'm out of friends and this is a huge request." Mike said he would help if he could. "Write this down, 'route 7 box 221.' Can you remember that? It's the Woodburn address of my granddad. He's dead and the place is about to be sold for a big farm or something. Tomorrow morning will you drive down there and get a case out of the old barn for me? My dad hid it under the second layer of hay bales in the back of the loft. It's a metal business case. Grandpa never knew it was there, and dad has taken the information to his grave. I don't know what's in it, but I think it's a shit load of money, or something really valuable, maybe the payment for a bootleg shipment of booze. I'll split it with you 50/50. I heard that Paul Levine has been tearing up the countryside looking for it for years. He trashed dad's place trying to figure out who has it. It must have been his dad and some cronies who stole it in the first place. I never heard how my dad got it. It's almost like a pirate story. Now no one knows where it's buried. Fortunately mom's cancer claimed her four years ago, so she wasn't hurt. I've been here in Salem for almost two years, so I have been safe too.

Will you do it for me?" he asked urgently.

"Yeah, I can drive down and take a look, but I'm not about to get tangled up in anything illegal, or part of your trouble. I'll give you a call when I get back." Mike was ready to hang up.

"No, let me call you." Ernie hung up without a farewell.

As Mike mulled over the prospects of a clandestine favor, he was terribly aware that it was not righteous because it blurred the shine from his relationship with the new commitment to God. It made him feel a little sick to his stomach, like hill 266. He called Marty to say he was suddenly feeling upset and would need to take the night off. He clocked out, then took a bus to his mom's place to borrow her car. A little after midnight he was at an all-night service station north of Woodburn, asking directions.

"Just follow the Molalla road about a mile. I think that is route 7. Who're you lookin' for?" the attendant asked, "Maybe I know them."

"Oh we're trying to find a farm that will let us hunt geese," Mike lied.

"You might try at Franklins when it gets light. They have the big white barn. You can't miss it."

Mike thanked the helpful man, or perhaps he was just bored at this hour and thankful for anyone who would shoot the breeze.

It took some extra care trying to find a mailbox number in the dark. Finally he found the right road, then found the right address. He drove past it, looking for any sign of others. About a quarter mile up the road he turned around and drove past it again. He pulled off the road and walked back to the driveway. There were no tire tracks in the mud, no footprints either.

He was careful to stay on the grassy edge of the driveway that headed for the barn that looked neglected and rundown. There was not a light visible anywhere, even in the distant houses. His heart was beating rapidly.

Mike turned on his flashlight briefly to find the ladder to the hayloft. In the deep shadows, he found a pile of old hay bales and struggled to find the back of it. Slowly he felt around the bales to detect a booby trap or warning wire of any sort. There was none. He moved a bale out of the way and repeated the process on the next one, and the next. "This is crazy," he was muttering to himself when his hand touched a cold surface. Carefully he explored it, too, for any booby-trap, until he found a hand grip and slowly eased the case out. "Damn! Now what?" He carefully made his way back to the ladder and then to the car. The serious shakes didn't start until he was back headed north on the highway. He decided the most prudent action would be to keep the case away from his house, so he stopped at the school's security office, and placed the case in his gym locker under a sweaty towel and covered by the gym bag. It wasn't as secure as a safety deposit box in the bank, but it was hidden and locked; the best he could do with what he had. Any casual glance would not see it there. That would have to do. He returned his mom's car, and caught a bus back to the school in time for his first class of the day. Then he waited to hear from Ernie.

Three days later the switchboard called him with a message: "Call Lieutenant French of the Portland police at Burnside 7-1735 extension 35."

He was mystified what this might be about, but because of Ernie's request, he was alert and on guard. He dialed the number. When he got through he asked, "Lt. French? This is Mike O'Malley returning your call."

"Yeah, O'Malley, let's see. Yeah, you are on my watch list." Mike wondered what the heck this might be about.

"Yeah, O'Malley, do you know an Ernest Carrel?"

"Yes, I do. Do you want to tell me what this is all about?"

"I'll ask the questions right now. When was the last time you saw him?"

"When we were in high school at Wilson, in '51."

"Are you sure about that? You can get in a lot of hurt giving false witness."

Now Mike was on full alert. If this man was a police officer he was a pretty shabby one, throwing around veiled threats. "I'm very sure. It was before he went into juvenile detention and I went to Korea."

"So, Mr. Vet-ran (he mispronounced the word into a slur), would you like to explain the card you just sent him? What does 'good news of great joy' mean? Did he ask you to do something for him?"

"Oh my goodness, it was a Christmas card. I wanted to tell him I am a candidate for the priesthood." That was true, but Mike was pretty sure the next answer wouldn't be.

"Yeah, your holiness, you want to explain then what the phone call was on the night of Sunday the 16th? Were you two talkin' about the Bingo game, or something bigger?" Fortunately, his careless question gave Mike time to come up with a plausible answer.

"I guess he got my work number off the Christmas card. He said he needed money and wanted to know if I would buy his old Ford. I told him I'm broke too, and he hung up. In fact,

# THE CORRUPTION OF FATHER MIKE

he didn't even say goodbye."

"How sad for you, altar boy. Hey O'Malley, what kind of car do you drive?"

"I suspect you have already checked with the DMV and know I've never had a car."

"Yeah, you know what else I know? I know you don't have a friend named Ernie either. He was killed outside his cell last night. Someone clocked him hard enough to break his little neck, and I want to know what you had to do with that."

There was a long silence before Mike said, "Lieutenant French, I called you as a courtesy. May I speak to your supervisor?"

"Yeah O'Malley, I'm watching you, and you can kiss my supervisor ass." The line went dead.

Mike hung up the phone with trembling hands. This was even worse than he could imagine it to be. Ernie was dead, and no one in the world knew that he had in his possession a mysterious case that could not be returned to a former owner. This was like one of those value oriented moral dilemmas. Right now he thought it would have been smarter to say "No" and stay at work instead of answering a friend's last request. "And now Ernie is dead!" he thought with tears in his eyes. Finally he decided to try to bury his thoughts in his studies.

On New Year's Eve, most of the buildings were closed, but he still had to lock the dorms. As he made his way past the parlor of the women's dorm, a voice called, "Mike do you have a minute?" It was Gloria. Of course he stopped to see what she needed.

Her face was more serious than he had seen before. She looked down at her feet, then into his eyes. "Hi," she said softly.

"I just heard about it; is it true?"

"I'm not sure what you are asking. Is what true?" Mike wondered.

"Is it true that you signed an intent card to do the Master's Program for priesthood?"

Now he understood her distress. They had been on a couple social dates since the Sadie Hawkins evening. But that was two years ago, and they had never spoken about a serious relationship. "Yes, it's true. I had no idea you might be distressed by that."

"Of course I'm sad… for me. I thought we might be a perfect match. I know there has never been any romance, but that just made me care for you more. I think I love you, Mike. But if you become a priest…." She couldn't finish the thought. A tear traced down her cheek.

He was quiet for a moment, then said, "Gloria, you are a sweet friend, the best I have here. But my only priority is the studies." He shifted nervously.

"You haven't deceived me, Mike." Her chin quivered and she began to weep openly. "I did that to myself. I just so hoped it would come true." She turned and walked to the stairs, leaving Mike to ponder again the opportunity overlooked.

Fr. James had carefully helped Mike choose his last quarter's schedule of classes. Geology 101 would satisfy his science requirement, and Logic would clean up the requirement for Math, and a Community Planning Program in Suburban Design finished his Sociology Minor. He even had enough room to sign up for a Renaissance Painters class. It might fill the void in art appreciation. The one that seemed to interest him most was the assignment to design the ideal new suburb.

# THE CORRUPTION OF FATHER MIKE

When this final quarter was finished, with a Bachelor degree with a major in Psychology, he would be ready to begin the Master's program with a summer intensive.

One morning he was wearily returning to his room after a night of study. His bed was a promise of rest for a few hours. When he approached his door, however, he was surprised to see it open, ajar. Cautiously he peered in to find his closet open and the drawers askew. Someone had thrown his mattress aside, and gone through his things, looking for.... There was little doubt in his mind what they might be looking for. He called Marty to report the vandalism, and asked if there had been any unusual traffic during the morning. He didn't expect anyone sneaky enough to find his fourth floor room of being careless enough to be seen.

In February, Fr. James approached Mike about a special opportunity to be a student Intern at Legacy Good Samaritan Hospital in the juvenile psych ward commonly known as the fifth floor. They needed a male intake processor. Mike had experience from his junior year, and they were requesting him again. If he was willing, he could drop the Art subject and get credit for his field placement activity instead. It would strengthen his major.

"Will it interrupt my security job?" Mike asked.

"No, but it might change your sleep pattern. They want someone who can work mornings, seven to noon. Apparently their intake of troubled youth is primarily at night. They need to be evaluated and processed as soon as possible."

"I'll bet they would agree to seven till ten, since it's a volunteer job," Mike negotiated. "That way I could still get back to Geology at eleven."

It would be a busy four months, but if everyone played fair, and the buses stayed on time, he could check the buildings for the final time at 6:00 in the morning, get to the cafeteria to make a couple scrambled egg sandwiches to go, catch the 6:20 bus on Willamette Blvd, and get within a block of Legacy Good Sam Hospital. He was at his desk by seven, and reminding any critics that he was a student volunteer. They loved his attitude.

Mike missed a Community Planning class and had to take an afternoon to visit the Multnomah County building department. The engineer, James Herald, who had led the class, had to give approval to his initial suburban expansion design. "This is a very interesting concept," he said as he looked at the sketch. "Obviously your intent is not to serve the inner city poor, but to create senior housing. I like that a lot. Pointing to a corner, he asked, "Does this say 'clinic?'"

"Yes sir," Mike responded. And the one next to it is a club house with a café."

Actually, Mike had not focused on just one group or age segment to serve, but tried to make a wholesome and safe community.

"You might want to think about parking codes, and add a little more of that. Do you have a name for it, like Portland West Hills, or Sunset Vista?" Mike grinned sheepishly. "I'm not the most creative guy. When we were singing Christmas carols, I thought about a name, 'Venite Village.' You know, 'Venite ado remus.' It means 'come,' or 'beckon.' Since it is an imaginary development, I thought any name would do."

"It's a catchy name. It sort of reminds me of the girl in high school I never got to meet." They both enjoyed a chuckle.

But on the bus ride back to school, Mike was thinking about how many "V" women's names he could come up with. Vicky, Verna, Veronica… but no Venite. "What the heck," he thought, "I still like the name 'Venite Village.'"

The schedule Mike had taken on was grueling. Those who were working with him admired his fortitude and dependability. He did renegotiate with the hospital. If he had no admissions to process by nine o'clock, he would return to school for study or rest. The afternoon admissions could take care of the few that came in during the day.

The juggling challenge got through February, and then March. Mike's biggest challenge was memorizing the geologic time periods, and identifying tiny fossils from each. April, rainy as ever, surrendered to May and finally Mike could see the light at the end of his tunnel.

He arrived at the hospital one Monday morning, anticipating the same easy list he had recently enjoyed. Instead there were three admissions, all police involvements. The first was a young man arrested at a graduation party. "Name?" Mike asked routinely. "Age?" "Home address?" "Doctor's name?" "School? And grade?" The questions were becoming so automatic he hardly listened. He perused the accompanying police report, if any, and chose a counselor who would begin the official clinical process.

The second was a very cute seventeen year old, who had been arrested at the Benson Hotel with two older men. The petite girl had been drinking, and was on her way up to the rooms when the police confronted her. The charges were a minor under the influence and suspicion of prostitution. Her brown eyes didn't move from his as the questions were answered. Those eyes were mesmerizing; he felt drawn to her. "Yeah, stupid," he thought to himself, "that's her stock in trade! That's what she is good at!" But he knew he would remember those eyes.

The third was a young woman, considerably overweight, who had apparently taken a substantial amount of sedatives in the attempt to take her own life. Medics had cleaned out her stomach, but the likelihood of her trying it again was high. She never looked at Mike as the questions were answered and she was assigned to a counseling physician.

He was making his way out of the hospital, when he heard someone call his name. "Hey O'Malley!" Turning to find the source, he recognized Brad Phillips, his old wrestling competitor. "I thought that was you." In a gray suit and blue tie, he looked very professional. "What are you doing here on the fifth floor?" He held out a sincere handshake.

Happily accepting his hand, recognizing the strength of his grip, Mike shared his purpose here.

"You're going to be a priest?" Brad asked with joy. "That is fantastic! I'm really glad for you." Then he told Mike that he also was finished with Law School at Willamette. "I passed the bar exam last year and the Prosecuting Attorney's Office here in Portland has given me a chance. I'm just working my way in, but the future seems very promising. Who would have guessed that the two heavy weights of Wilson High would turn out to be a priest and a lawyer?"

They did a bit of the catch up conversation, then Mike asked, "What are you doing here on my fifth floor?" He chuckled playfully.

"Oh they give me the scrap stuff nobody else wants. I'm

here to take a deposition of a woman arrested last night at the Benson."

"Leanne Levine?" Mike asked in disbelief.

"The very same."

"But she's just a seventeen year old, living with her grandparents," Mike said, repeating the information he had gathered.

"Yeah, she put a Full Nelson on you with that line." Brad shook his head. "She is twenty two, and looking to get before a Juvenile Judge. The worst she would get is probation. Her dad is one of the biggest crooks in Portland, and slipperier than a slug. She has never had a driver's license so she can only show her Parkrose High School I.D. It does say she is seventeen… still. We are convinced she has been in on several of her dad's schemes, but there isn't enough proof to charge her. I'm betting this one will be the same. There is no proof she was drinking alcohol, and she was arrested before they got to the room. It is no crime to be standing with someone in the lobby with all your clothes on. She'll walk away from this one too." As he gave Mike one of his business cards, Mike thought it would be great when he had one to exchange. "Are you going to stay in the Portland area?" Brad asked.

"Plans are still unfolding," Mike answered. "But things have sure worked out well so far. I'll stay in touch." He actually meant it.

Graduation was a marvelous experience for Mike. The Field House was adorned with colorful drapes and fake plants. The basketball hoops were raised almost out of sight. It would be easy to forget the many lost competitions to other schools in this gym. Today however, was a celebration of victory! Over a hundred women and men had completed their Bachelor of

Arts Degree and were moving on to larger challenges. For Mike, having his mother in attendance was a deep satisfaction. She had never in her adult life had something to believe in. When she saw her son stride across that platform and receive his degree with honors, she knew he had done it alone, and she believed he had done it for her!

While classmates were planning celebrative vacation trips, he looked forward to a dinner out with his mom, and a bus ride to Madigan for his annual hearing check-up. In three years there had been little change. Then it would be back to his fourth floor dorm room and preparation for another summer intensive. He would dig deeply into the Gospel of John. In the fall it would be studies in worship, counseling, homilies, and the Sacraments. Round and round it goes, like children riding painted ponies.

# St Joseph's

In the middle of his second year of the Master's program, Mike received a phone call from the Bishop's office, requesting a conversation at his earliest convenience. Since he had not recently struck anyone with his batons, he couldn't imagine what it might be about. Fr. James answered that question for him. He actually visited Mike in the Security Office after the 9:00 lock-up. When Mike saw him open the door, he understood immediately that this was not a social call, but a matter of great importance to the Registrar, whom he knew as a trusted friend and scholar.

"Mike, you have already guessed that this is an unusual situation of the highest importance," his gentle friend began. "I am going to trust you with some information that must remain confidential. I am tonight, not speaking for the University of Portland, but for the Bishop of the Archdiocese of Portland. Do I have your pledge to privacy?"

"Of course," Mike said, deeply touched by the formality of Fr. James.

"When we think death is the worst interruption to our lives, we run into some calamity like this and know it is even worse. Our priest at Newberg has been caught molesting a boy, perhaps several. When confronted by furious parents, the priest got into his car and simply drove away. He was a coward as well as a lecherous man. We are not sure where he might be hiding, but police are searching."

"Here is the request the Bishop is bringing to you tonight, obviously in a state of emergency. There is no other priest in Newberg. A retired priest has agreed to man the parish for two weeks, serving the mass and hearing confessions, but his health is so weak, that it is the most he can offer. There might be some priest in another Archdiocese, but at the moment that is unclear. You, my stalwart friend, have completed half of your Master's studies. Are you willing to accept a Student Interim assignment to St. Joseph's, while continuing your work here? Your ordination would happen when you finish next year, so you would be serving under good supervision, probably from me."

"I have seen you address great challenge in your time here, using the hours of a day more ingenious than most could imagine. In many ways, the Newberg Parish would be no less challenging, in other ways, you would have a more fragile experience of walking with an entire community in shock. You would be provided a vehicle to commute back and forth. There would, of course, be a stipend." Mike's head was in a spin, knowing that this was an ultimate honor, and also a supreme challenge.

"When do you need an answer?" Mike asked. "How long do I have to pray about this?"

"Let's pray about this right now; then you can tell me tomorrow how you are feeling. If you would like, the Bishop will pray with you also." They bowed, Fr. James held Mike's hand, saying, "O God, our Father, we ask your help so to live that we shall always be on the right way. Tonight we pray for your church at Newberg, and the great pain they must be feeling. Guide us in every choice which life brings us so that we may always choose the right way. Purify our ambitions so that we may set our hearts only on the things which please you. Control our thoughts that we may never linger on the wrong things, or stray down the pathways in which they ought not to go. Guard our lips so that no word which would shame ourselves or hurt another may ever pass through them. Direct our actions, so that we may always work with diligence, act in honor, and live in kindness. Help us also always to be willing to accept your help when you offer it to us, so that we may always take your high and holy way, in Jesus' precious name, Amen."

Fr. James would have released his hand, but Mike held on. He looked directly into the Registrar's eyes. "You wouldn't have asked me to do this if you had grave doubts about my ability, and we have prayed for God's guidance. Why should I not agree to this. Please tell the Bishop the words from Isaiah : 'Whom shall I send, and who will go for us?' Then I said, 'Here am I! Send me.' Why should I make a crisis worse by hesitating because of my fears? If you think I can do it, and you promise to stand with me, we must say 'Yes!'" Once again, Fr. James found tears in Mike's eyes, and in his as well.

Suddenly, Mike's life was in high gear... no, overdrive! He met with the Bishop, which was a thrilling moment of blessing. He was complimented for his military service, as though that had something to do with the current situation, and his exemplary academic work. He was also made aware of the expectations of the parish , which if he could meet, he would be a winner of another medal. He met with his three professors; since they were all priests themselves, they bought into the emergency and vowed their assistance where appropriate. Then, everyone held their breath.

Mike drove the '51 Chevy, which belonged to the Newberg church, having called each of the parish leaders, inviting them to a moment of prayer. When he parked in the St. Joseph's parking lot, he tried to envision a group of Christians with God's shining presence upon them. He imagined the flame of the Holy Spirit over the church and her people. There were several other cars there. In his heart he felt a message: "You are their priest, their hope." He walked into the small sanctuary with as much courage as he could muster. Each person received a handshake and a direct look. Mike tried to remember names.

When they were introduced, he asked if they would join him in prayer. He especially needed it, but made sure the prayer was nurturing for the congregation. Then he asked for their expectations, having no priest but a seminary student to lead them. Conversation was brisk and honest, with much laughter. He tried to outline his schedule as best he could. He would be in the parish mornings Monday through Fridays, and all weekend; he would be in school afternoon and evenings, but needed them to know that during the week, he was also building security until midnight through the end of the school year.

Finally he was asked about his military service. He told them just the important points, Yokosuka, Korea, bronze star, a silver star, a purple heart and two hearing aids. "The last two make it pretty easy for folks to sneak up behind me, but when they do it in love, it has been O.K." There was laughter, and more appreciation when he asked them to close this initial meeting with shared prayers. Many had affirmative words; then Mike closed with another heartfelt prayer. They understood that while limited in experience, this man was truly a priest at heart, and the strongest leader they had ever welcomed.

Two Sundays later they saw that leadership in its first demonstration. Fr. James offered to drive them to St. Joseph's, so he could share the morning. He also began the liturgy, read the scripture selections, and then introduced Mike as their new student interim priest. While Fr. James wore the Stole and Maniple of a priest, Mike wore a simple surplice over the clerical collar the Bishop had presented. He took a deep breath and began his homily.

"Thank you for such a cordial welcome. It's an important start, isn't it? We all know what it's like to be a stranger in the crowd, like being at the train station when everyone has someone to greet them but you. You watch other people sharing a hug, a kiss, a handshake, but you feel alone. A couple years ago I was at Mount Angel abbey. We were taking a break and I knew no one there. To be fair, I work night security at the school so I haven't been able to join groups or social activities where I would meet others. I stood there while friends met and laughed together. I stood there with my white Styrofoam cup of coffee, not knowing what to do. You know, after you say 'hello' to that steaming cup of coffee there's not much conversation. Yeah, you can stand there making little designs on the cup with your thumbnail. But if you're not careful, you could tear off a corner of the bottom, and spring a leak to your utter shock and horror." A ripple of laughter was shared. "Then, you not only have the problem of feeling alone and self-conscious, now you are faced with holding a stream of steaming coffee, looking for some place to dump it. Before you just felt awkward; now with coffee running down your arm you feel like an idiot!" The congregation responded with laughter.

"That moment was nothing compared to what some of you are feeling this morning, I know. You look around the church and wonder what is going to happen. Feeling anger, or disappointment, or discouragement, you may be wondering, 'What am I doing here?' I know it is one thing to have a social hiccup with a Styrofoam cup, and a completely different moment when in shock and betrayal, you have no idea what the future holds, or you lack a sense of belonging or purpose."

"The Epistle reading this morning is from the letter to the Ephesians. There was a time when some of the early Christians desperately needed a word of affirmation. They needed a word about their identity. They needed to know that the challenge that was being required of them was really important and worth the sacrifice being demanded of them. That is why the affirmations of the first three chapters of Ephesians is so important. In one way or another this text says, 'You belong – you really belong.'"

"Once upon a time there was a little boy, You know that the Irish really love stories like this. who had a mark on the back of his hand. He had had that mark as long as he could remember. Some said it was only an ugly blotch. Others mocked it saying it was the result of his mother's sin. Still others looked at it and saw, when they turned his hand a certain way, the image of a bird, a dove. The little boy was an orphan . He was one of the thousands of homeless abandoned children in a great South American city."

"His name was Roberto. He was thin and scrawny, dirty

and a pathetic specimen of a child. His eyes were dark and luminous – like the eyes of a wounded animal. Roberto could not remember a home or a father and mother. His earliest memories were of hunger, loneliness, dirt and fighting for anything to eat. He slept in a cardboard box with rolled up newspaper to keep warm. He was like an ugly shadow, like a frail, hollow-eyed leper. No one heard his sobs, nor dried his tears."

"Now I want to tell you something about Roberto that he himself did not know. He does have a home; he does have a father and mother who long for him; he does belong. When he was just a baby he was kidnapped by a ruthless gang who demanded a fortune in ransom. The parents paid the money, but the kidnappers did not honor their promise to return Roberto. Instead he was dumped along with the other refuse of the city. The heart-sick parents posted his picture; the newspapers carried the story. But Roberto was swept into the discards of the city. Other children may have helped him. So near starvation, he must have struggled desperately, because he did survive. There was no honor, no dignity, no security, just a long struggle for something to eat. Now and then Roberto would be troubled by a reoccurring dream. In his dream, he imagined a home, a mother singing to him, food, laughter, a family nurturing him. But always he awoke to the sordid, tragic, painful, real world that he presumed was the total reality instead of the dream."

"We know of course, that the fading dreams that Roberto pushed from his mind was a link to reality. But how could Roberto know that? Who would ever tell him?"

"You just heard Fr. James read from a very old document written to the Robertos – to those who feel cut off – homeless

– of no value – confused. It is a letter that speaks of home – a place where you belong. It speaks of one who deeply cares, and it speaks of an identity that is given."

"The amazing thing about the document is that the first three chapters, written in the Greek language, appear in the affirmative mood. Doesn't that sound like something a second year seminarian would want to say? That means it affirms something that has already been done for us, given to us,. It affirms a relationship that already exists."

"Of course you know by now that I am talking about the book of Ephesians – the first three chapters. Listen again to the verses which speak to our identity and calls us into a new future: 'Blessed be the God and Father of our Lord Jesus Christ, who has blessed us in Christ with *every spiritual blessing* in the heavenly places…'"

"That is something God has already done for us. It is affirmative! He has blessed us with every spiritual blessing; the word blessing literally means a special wonderful gift. Why should I eat out of garbage cans or steal scraps of food when I have been blessed with every spiritual blessing? Why don't I claim my heritage?"

"Did you hear verse 4? '….even as he chose us in him before the foundations of the world, that we should be holy and blameless before him.' How can that be? We are told that before the foundations of the world, we have been chosen to be holy – and blameless before God! How can Roberto believe that?"

"This amazing letter tells us that we are not only blessed, chosen, but also destined in love to be God's children, and that accepting this identity actually even *praises him*!

Do you get the picture now? Here is Roberto in loneliness, pain , and tragic despair. There are people who love him, who really have a home for him, who have an inheritance for him."

"You know that the Irish love long stories, so there is more that I want to tell you. As Roberto grew up his story became more tragic still. The simple theft of a scraps of food became an assault to gain more. He joined a gang that did terrible things. He was involved with violence and terrible acts of cruelty, until he was arrested, even for crimes he didn't commit; and because he had no defense, he was sentenced to prison. The doors slammed shut behind him; it was like slamming a coffin lid. He had an inheritance but he was rotting and dying in prison. He was loved and valued – but he didn't know it. Now the only reality to Roberto seemed to be that of the crowded violent, corrupt, prison in which death seemed inevitable."

"Let us imagine that Roberto had a friend who happened to be looking through some old newspapers on a remote shelf of the prison library. The friend happens to read the story of the kidnapped boy who had a strange mark on the back of his hand in the shape of a bird. Let's imagine that this friend really cared for Roberto, and broke the news to him of who he really was. Of course he couldn't believe it. But then the friend helped get the news to the family. They came to the prison to see for themselves."

"They waited outside until their son came through the door. Of course they didn't recognize one another. They were shocked. He was so much older, he looked terrible, hardened, cynical. But still they took his hand, and saw the birth mark. They spoke his name and he didn't respond. Then the mother remembered the old song she sang in the nursery; once again she sang it quietly. Suddenly there was a look of recognition. Roberto remembered the dream. 'Mother! Father!' Roberto had found his home! With the help of his family there was a new trial with a sound defense, new information for the judge. His sentence was reduced; he was set free, and had a new life. That is the amazing witness of scripture! When condemnation seems certain, God speaks the word of affirmation, deliverance, and grace. He tells us that we are no longer prisoners, or nobodies. We are citizens of the kingdom , members of his family. That is not something that we do; it is something that God has already done for us. It is the affirmative word. It is accomplished. Listen with me to the second chapter verse one: 'And you he made alive, when you were dead through the trespasses and sins, in which you once walked...' And then the scripture adds this amazing affirmation: 'So then you are no longer strangers and sojourners, but you are fellow citizens with the saints and members of the household of God...'"

"Wouldn't that be great if that were the happy ending to Roberto's story? But we know that when he got home, was bathed and clothed in fresh clean clothes, there was still part of the old Roberto alive. Yes, he was no longer a no-body. He is free, but he must now become the son he is. He will be tempted to steal, as he has always done. He will feel the call to the old life. He may even want to run away, to reject their goodness. He is a beloved, and valued son; now he must become a loved and valued son."

"This is the great Biblical pattern. We see it in this great book of Ephesians. The first three chapters deal with what God has done. Here are some of the loftiest and most powerful language in all the Bible. It is the affirmative mood! God has done it!"

"The second half of the book makes a shift. The verb changes from the affirmative to the imperative – from what God has done, to what we are to do. Now I know I sound like a second year seminarian. Hold on for just a little more."

"Listen to chapter four verse one: 'I therefore, a prisoner for the Lord, beg you to live a life worthy of the calling to which you have been called...' You were dead – God made you alive – that is affirmative. 'Put off your old nature which belongs to your former manner of life... and put on the new nature, created after the likeness of God in true righteousness and holiness.' If we don't spend time in the first three chapters of Ephesians the Christian faith becomes nagging and a whole lot of fuss, just rules and regulations, 'shoulds' and 'oughts', and no joy. If you don't deal with chapters four through six, God is just a big sugar daddy, and religion becomes a soft dessert with no muscle, responsibility or challenge. You are a child of God, now become a child of God. You are a new person in Christ, therefore become a new person in Christ."

"We affirm God's action. We are no longer strangers – we are fellow citizens with the saints and members of the household of God. We are the Church - now become the Church! That is God's great challenge to this church in the months ahead. It is to affirm our identity, and move into it. We must claim with excitement, and joy, and confidence, the forgiveness and healing God is providing. We must realize that Jesus Christ is present with us in this church. He is the chief cornerstone, in whom the whole structure is joined together and grows into a holy temple, in whom we are to build together and form a dwelling place of God in the Spirit."

"I heard a story recently about a family that was driving

along on a Sunday afternoon ride. The children in the back seat started yelling for their father to stop the car. "Daddy, there is a little kitty back there. Can't we take him home?" The father replied 'No,' and drove on a bit, but the volume was cranking up, 'Please daddy, it's so wet and cold, it might die. Please.' 'No, I said, we don't need a cat!' And he drove on."

"You know where this is going don't you? The children began to cry louder. Dad stopped and backed up and saw the scrawny, mangy, watery-eyed, pitiful excuse for a cat there on the side of the road, a crumpled sack near it was evidence of how it had gotten there. Someone had discarded it. He took a towel out of the trunk, not wanting to even touch the scruffy thing, wrapped it up and placed it in the trunk, and they took it home. The children gave it milk and food. They combed it and cared for it. Gradually the appearance of the cat changed. It gained weight. Its coat became soft and beautiful. It was no longer terrified around people. One day while the dad was reading his newspaper, the cat walked into the room, and rubbed up along the side of his shoe, purring loudly. He reached down and stroked its head."

"Friends, I have a question. Was that the same cat or not? It makes a difference when you are no longer a stray on the side of the road, but instead have found a home. We are the church – now we must become the church powerful and strong. The final words from this ancient letter help us accomplish that task. Listen."

Mike moved away from the pulpit to kneel on the floor in front of the congregation. He spread wide his arms and quoted from chapter six: "'Finally, be strong in the Lord and in the strength of his might. Put on the whole armor of God, that you may be able to stand against the wiles of the devil. For we are not contending against the world rulers of this present darkness, against the spiritual host of wickedness in the heavenly places. Therefore take the whole armor of God, that you may be able to withstand in the evil day, and having done all, to stand. Stand, therefore, having girded your loins with truth, and having put on the breastplate of righteousness, and having shod your feet with the equipment of the gospel of peace; besides all these, taking the shield of faith, with which you can quench all the flaming darts of the evil one. And take the helmet of salvation, and the sword of the Spirit which is the word of God.'" The inside of the church was breathlessly silent.

Mike finally lowered his arms inviting the congregation to pray with him as he continued to kneel before them. "O Great and Gracious Lord God, we accept that we are no longer strangers, but your loved and chosen ones. Help us now move forward as the household of God. We go forward in confidence and commitment, for we know whose hand is leading us, and whose divine love is sustaining us in Jesus powerful name. Amen."

Fr. James announced the offering and prepared the elements for communion. After the prayer, he served the host, while Mike served the cup. A benediction concluded the service. Many folks wanted to greet them both, but several paused to tell Mike how masterful they felt the homily had been presented: "You dealt with our problem without mentioning it once!" "We loved the sermon, you helped us with a terrible problem. I know this is going to work wonders." "We've never had a seasoned priest hold our attention so well." "I'm eager to be back next week. It's been a while since I felt that way."

On their way back to the school, Fr, James had some helpful words and much praise for the way Mike had led the worship hour. "Do you think you can do that week after week?" he asked.

"Right now I think they are pretty focused on getting through Christmas." Mike answered. "That should be pretty easy. Fr. Lopez offered to stop by the security office each Monday night to chat about the following Sunday's scripture. That will be a colossal help." Mike was still for a bit, then added, "If I can remain free from the other agenda, other than being a healing agent, I think I'll be fine."

"Speaking of the security office reminds me," Fr. James said, "Mr. Powers tells me you have one of the lockers at the weight room." A chill passed down Mikes back. "There is going to be some remodeling down there, and new lockers put in. If you could get your things out by the first of the year it would be helpful." This was the first time in quite a while that Mike had to think about that cursed case. "I'll get on it this week," he promised. But in his thoughts was the question, "What in the world can I do with it?"

He tried to forget the problem by burying his attention in study work. But it persisted. The conclusion was only gradually revealed. At first he wanted to simply throw the darned thing in the garbage; but that would be so irresponsible, and there was a tiny part of him that was curious what might be in the case. He thought about burying it in a plastic bag; but that only postponed the inevitable. He would need to deal with it out of some respect for Ernie. But he needed help and could think of no other person he wanted to involve. He recalled the parable of the ten talents. The unworthy servant had buried his

# THE CORRUPTION OF FATHER MIKE

one talent in fear, and received the Master's ire for not at least putting it in a bank. "That was the very best thing that could happen," Mike reasoned. If the contents of the case could be in the bank, it would be safe. But that in itself presented new problems: whose name should be on the account? "Not mine," Mike shuddered. "How could I walk into the bank with anything of value?"

Finally, in the middle of the night the idea was formed. Mike would get a business license with a tax number, and open a bank account at Columbia Federal, in the name of Venite Village, with his name on the signature card. Then he could pay an attorney that he knows to make the deposit. He was amazed at how easy it all happened. Even the snaps on the case were unlocked, if somewhat stiff. Brad needed a little more information about the origin and purpose of the money. When Mike explained that an eccentric citizen who insisted on remaining anonymous had no criminal record or ties, and the money in question was completely legitimate. He simply wanted to start a business. Brad agreed, but warned Mike that his hourly rate was $25 dollars an hour. He should be prepared for a $50 dollar bill. When they opened the case to examine the contents, they found a large stack of $10,000 dollar U.S. Treasury Bearer Bonds from 1938, still with their interest coupons intact. "I think $50 would be about right," Mike agreed in a whisper. Both men were speechless in the presence of this huge cache.

When Brad had the bank recount the bonds they agreed, there were 313 bonds worth $3,130,000 dollars, an additional $1,565,00 dollars of interest made the total deposit $4,695,000! Now the challenge would be to use it in a way that honored Ernie's memory. He hadn't died for it, but because of it.

At 9:15 promptly, Fr. Lopez peeked in the security room, asking, "Am I late?"

"You are very much on time and so very welcome here!" Mike said happily. "I need your help, and wisdom."

"That's not the story I heard. I was told you did a champion job, ministering to a hurt congregation and winning their hearts with your sincerity. Can you follow it with another fine Sunday?"

Mike produced a sheet of paper. "I've been thinking I need to be working on more than next week's homily. Here's my outline for the rest of Advent:

December 15  Matthew 1:8-25 "When Joseph Woke Up"
Joseph's problem – the pregnancy
Joseph is a just man – divorce her quietly instead of stoning.
Joseph dreamed – don't argue with an angel – Do not fear
Joseph woke up, obediently, he apologizes and reconciles, and invitation for us also.

December 22nd Luke 1:26-55 "When Mary Spoke Up"
Listen to Mary's question: How can this be?
Mary's personal commitment, Behold I am a doule (servant;)
Word of Praise: Magnificat
Mary spoke for Justice and Righteousness
One final word, spoken to the infant Jesus, unheard, of personal love.

December 24th Matthew 2:1-12 "Christmas Intentions"
God's intention is to bring his light into our darkness; "Gift

## THE CORRUPTION OF FATHER MIKE

of the Magi"

Herod intends to destroy

Wise men intend to worship, Van Dyke's "Other Wise Man."

They talked until Mike had to make his 10:00 building check. As Fr. Lopez was leaving, he assured Mike that he was giving a very positive representation of the school. "We have many graduates who are wishing they could duplicate your ministry. I'll see you in class."

Mike's second Sunday at St. Joseph's went just as well as the first, much to his relief. A group of parishioners lingered to invite him to a local restaurant for lunch. He saw it for what it was; another opportunity to minister to these hurt and confused folks.

The small talk was mostly about the smooth transition Mike was accomplishing, and their praise for his efforts to relate so genuinely. Finally the real issue emerged. John Rice, perhaps the most stalwart of the group acted as spokesman. "I suspect you have seen me hanging around the church since you arrived. I don't want you to take this wrong, but since all this heartache started, I've been having trouble getting it out of my mind. I keep wishing I had paid closer attention, seen some warning signs, kept an eye on the kids better. Now that it's too late, I'm afraid I'm having trouble trusting anyone." He was quiet for a moment, then added, "Even you." He looked into Mike's eyes, then down at the table. A couple of other heads nodded in agreement.

A woman said quickly, "Oh we don't mean to put any of this on you for goodness sake. It's like we are flinching whenever our kiddies are out of sight at the church."

Another man said, "John expressed it well for us. It's not blame so much as a breakdown of trust. We love our priest, but we don't know what to do with this misgiving feeling."

Mike realized the dichotomy of the situation; they wanted him to say something to ease their broken relationship with him. "I hope that in time that sense of trust, and respect will return. I'll do my best to work on that. Until then," he took a big breath, "how about doing something that might ease your anxiety? How about installing some of those new security cameras that are pretty cheap. We are putting them in all the dorms and offices at school. It's a practical way to make sure security is working. I wonder if you would feel better if there was an eye in the priest's study, the vestry, and maybe a couple in the rectory."

"How much do you think that would cost us?" John asked.

"I'm only guessing, but I think you could have four installed for about $300 dollars.

Everyone was quiet for a moment. "We've been saving up some money for some new tables in the community center so we could play Bingo. Maybe if we could use it for security…" She didn't finish her thought. Another silence waited for Mike's suggestion.

"Well, if you guys are asking for my thoughts, here they come", Mike said with his typical grin. "I think you should do anything you need to do to restore your confidence in your church, and by that I mean in your priest. If you believe the catechism classes need chaperones, let's recruit some grandmas to bring cookies for each class and they can remain until each child is picked up. If the security cameras would do it, for goodness sake, spend the money. Then, when you start seeing for yourselves that I am trustworthy, let's have a Box Social some Sunday afternoon to raise the money for those tables and chairs."

"Do you think we could get new chairs, too?" a woman asked.

Mike smiled, understanding that the trauma of the betrayal of their priest was extreme; it was not permanent. They would heal; they would forgive, eventually. "We are the church of Jesus Christ! Together we will do great things, chairs included." Laughter concluded their time together.

Mike's estimates were spot on. The security cameras were installed for $295 dollars, and the Box Social that was attended by most of the residents of Newberg, brought in over $600 dollars, enough for tables, and chairs for sure. Mr. Rice was a former Postmaster, as it turned out and he received each quarter the General Services Administration pamphlet of auction items being offered by the government. There was usually lots of office stuff, including tables and chairs. He promised to bring it to Mike as soon as it arrived.

St. Joseph's Church enjoyed Mike's leadership for almost two years. When it was time to say "goodbye," he reminded them that he had only been a student interim priest. They had both grown during their time together, in trust and respect. Attendance at mass had almost tripled; they had a part time secretary in the office and a paid organist. Mike graduated from the seminary with the respect of the faculty who used him as a model of what could be done both scholastically, and personally. St. Joseph's used him as an example of how healing and fresh confidence can come from even a student interim.

# Blessed Sacrament

The Bishop's office called him on a blustery January day asking if he could be available for an important meeting. When the day came, Mike wasn't sure if his excitement was from knowing he had done well at Newberg, or from the curiosity of not knowing where he might be sent next. Maybe it was a healthy mix of both. When he entered the Bishop's office he was happy to see Fr. James and Fr. Lopez, plus four other priests whom he had not met. The Bishop welcomed them and made introductions. Besides the two faculty members, two of the priests were on staff with a local congregation, and two were members of the Board of Priest's Assignment.

Finally the Bishop said to Mike, "We have had marvelous service from you as a young priest. The folks at Newberg are not real happy with me right now. But once again I am bringing to you a," he hesitated, looking at the men seated at the table, "situation that is unusual." Then reassuringly, he added, "Oh not the sort of crisis we had at St. Joseph's. Can we be in prayer?"

"Gracious Redeemer, we come to you as faithful servants, eager to hear and obey. Take from us, we pray, the laziness that will not learn, and the prejudice which cannot learn. Give us minds adventurous to think, memories strong to remember and wills resolute to build your Kingdom in our midst, in

Jesus' name, Amen." Mike wasn't sure how that prayer made him feel, so he set his attention on full alert.

"Mike, we did not ordain you at the conclusion of your seminary study as most were. We knew the St. Joseph congregation would love to keep you, but there is another alternative. Blessed Sacrament, right here in Portland is a parish with a great history. At one time it was the keystone church of the diocese; today it is weary and in need of a transfusion. Fr. McDonald is on staff there, offering Community Care, hospital and nursing home visits, funerals and memorial services, even weddings are his responsibility. Fr. Gregory is one of the best Christian Educators in the church. He is responsible for youth, college fellowship and small groups. He also gives supervision to the Education coordinator who is in charge of the day care and age level classes. Once again, it would be hard to find a more efficient crew as this. Our challenge is that Fr. Michaels, the Senior Priest who came to us from being Dean of the seminary is suddenly retiring, and their Personnel Committee has made it clear that they want a fresh and total shift in leadership. They want someone who can bring dynamic faith along with creative ideas." Mike was silent, his face pensive as he looked at Fr. James.

The Bishop continued, "We know this is not the sort of place a young priest hopes for. I asked Frs. Gregory and McDonald to be here to answer any questions you might have, and to assure you of their whole-hearted support." Mike looked at the two priests, each at least a couple decades older than him. "They each visited St Joseph's during this last month and heard the sort of preaching that our entire church is wanting. They are hopeful you will decide positively for Blessed Sacrament.

Do you have any questions for them?"

"No sir, I don't right now." He was off balance by the entire conversation.

There was a heavy silence until the Bishop quietly said, "Of course, I understand." After an uncomfortable pause, he said, "There are two other churches in the Archdiocese that are also in need of a priest."

"Oh, I am sorry to be unclear, sir. I certainly am not turning down anything that you think will be right for the church. I am overwhelmed by the compliment." Once again his eyes found his mentor. "I'd like to know what Fr. James feels about the potential of a fresh seminarian taking such a huge leap of responsibility." Once again he quietly waited.

"You are so right," Fr. James said. "Ordinarily this would be a preposterous suggestion. Not one seminarian in a hundred could be considered for Blessed Sacrament, even as weary as she is. But Mike, you are not one in a hundred, or even a thousand. How many grunts earn a Bronze Star for bravery? Perhaps a few. How many earn a Silver Star for throwing themselves on a grenade to save a tent-full of wounded brothers? Mike, you are the stuff heroes are made of, soldier or priest. I know Christ is so alive in you that this challenge will only be an opportunity for that celestial fire to burn more brightly. I know you can do this."

"Then everything else is just commentary," Mike said softly. Looking intently at the Bishop he said, "Bishop, if you want me to be at Blessed Sacrament, I am honored, humbled, and intimidated to say, 'Thank you for believing I can do it. I pledge you my very best effort.'"

Fr. Gregory came around the table with a large smile. As

he hugged Mike, he said, "I can't wait for the exciting change."

When Fr. McDonald came to him, Mike was given a hug and a kiss on the cheek. It would take a little effort, but he might get used to that.

The Bishop asked them to consecrate the moment with prayer. When all heads were bowed he prayed, "Holy and Wonderful Lord God, We give you thanks and praise that we can stand in the presence of true disciples. Help us find the sense of need which really makes us come to you for the things that you alone can provide, and the obedience which will really make us listen and obey in Jesus powerful name. Amen." As the Bishop shook Mike's hand he said, "My office is always available for any need you might have."

The transition was gentle and smooth thanks mainly to John Rice. He provided transportation, helped move the few boxes Mike had, and calmly represented a supportive congregation. Father Michaels had purchased a home in Beaverton so the rectory was vacant and Mike could move in at any time. They found a four year old Ford Crown Victoria parked in the garage with keys in the kitchen. Also in the kitchen they found Roberta Wiley, the housekeeper. She said it was her duty to clean the house and cook a lunch and supper for the priest and guests. It would take a while for Mike to adjust to that.

On Ash Wednesday, the Bishop ordained Mike and officially installed him as Senior Priest of Blessed Sacrament. Mike's mom and about twenty members of St. Joseph's attended with the congregation, and praised him for his will to serve God. Fr. James guided Mike through the vestry where all sorts of vestments were stored. While Mike found them unnecessary, Fr. James reminded him that the robes and stoles would be familiar items which the congregation would recognize and appreciate as Mike's office. "I need all the help I can get," Mike said appreciatively as he tried on several. He was a bit larger than the former priests but it made little difference to the vestments.

Remembering how well it worked at St. Joseph's, Mike asked Fr. McDonald, whom he intended to call 'Len' from now on, if he could invite a couple dozen of the congregation's leaders to a wine and cheese get-together on Saturday afternoon. Mike thought it would be much better to get to know a handful before he was challenged to meet so many. If the meeting went well, he planned to offer a monthly conversation until he knew most if not all the members.

He also called Fr. Lopez, requesting a few minutes on Friday afternoon to preview the homily. Mike thought it was a good beginning place, but needed a bit of reassurance. In touring the building he was most impressed with the cavernous old sanctuary. Including the balcony, that was no longer used, the seating capacity must have been 800 at least. The trustees had removed the back ten rows of pews in the nave to condense the attendance to make it look fuller. Then he waited for his first conversation.

"Thank you folks for making the effort to come out on a rainy afternoon. I'm thinking some of you want to meet the new priest, and some appreciate Mrs. Wiley's snack that she has graciously prepared. My hope is to learn the truth about Blessed Sacrament. I would love to hear what you would like to see changed, and what needs to be retained; remember that only the Bishop can amend the clergy staff. I have been warmly greeted by Frs. Len and Karl, and I hope to know all the staff as soon as possible. While you are thinking of what you would like to tell me, let me tell you a tiny bit about myself, because that's all there is to tell."

"I graduated from Wilson High and went right into the U.S. Army. My first station was Yokosuka Japan, where I learned the defensive use of batons, or night sticks. There were some who called me by the nickname 'Stix,' but I will not respond to that if you try to use it. Yes, it is true that I used the batons twice at the University, both times as a measure of last resort, and both times with disabling effect."

"I was sent to Korea, where I served in the 171st Artillery with a Browning Automatic. I was given a Commendation for Bravery, a Bronze Star, and a Commendation for Heroism and a Silver Star . The Japanese gave me a Commendation for breaking up a riot at the USO. I graduated from the University of Portland Seminary with Honors two years ago and have been serving as Student Interim at Newberg."

One of the men asked, "Were you placed on probation by the Provost?"

"No sir; please remind me of your name." The man said, "Ray Kellogg". Mike continued, "The Provost recommended probation to the Trustees, who chose not to act on it."

One of the women asked, "Do you still carry the night sticks?"

Mike smiled, "They are a little clumsy in a robe. But if you notice the Greek cross outside the rectory bedroom door, you will see that they are still available to me in an emergency." Wanting to change the direction, he said, "Now I have been open and honest with you, how would you answer the question: what would you like to see changed or retained at

Blessed Sacrament? And remember that no one is taking notes or names."

A woman answered immediately, " I think it is a shame that we are here in the heart of the city and ignore the needs of the poor around us."

"But we don't want to invite those who will take advantage of us;" Mr. Kellogg said, "we have been robbed at least a half a dozen times in the past two or three years. It seems sadly regular."

"We need more lights around the church and parking lot; that would help," another man offered.

Mike asked, "Have you ever thought about security cameras. They are much cheaper than replacing microphone equipment. Usually their presence is a warning to thieves."

"Yeah, but how expensive are they. You know this old church is just about to go under in debt." That was news to Mike.

"When the University installed them," he answered, "in the dorms and offices it was about a thousand dollars. But when St. Joseph's put theirs in, it was for less than three hundred." He didn't bother to tell them the ones at St. Joseph's was to watch the priest.

"I think we need more young people. Our congregation is faded gray." Everyone chuckled.

"Remember when we used to be very mission minded? We supported an orphanage in Guatemala. We don't hear much about missions anymore."

"This church is almost fifty years old and is more concerned about the acolyte's censer than a new family seeking a church home."

# THE CORRUPTION OF FATHER MIKE

Mike had noticed that Kent and Len (Frs. Gregory and McDonald) were silent, perhaps they were taking notes and names. He asked, "How about the catechism, youth, education programs?"

"Oh they are great!" Several nodded in agreement. Then one of the men who may have had a half of a glass too much said, "It all rests on the senior priest, Amigo. The buck stops right there. We need some heat in the kitchen. That's why we moved the other priests into apartments so you could enjoy the privacy of the rectory." That was also news to Mike. "For too long this place has been trying to live on yesterday's news, and historic traditions. It's on your shoulder's Fr. O'Malley. You may be our last hope."

Mike said with a happy smile, "I'd rather see me as the new beginning."

The conversation continued until the wine ran out and sunset had given way to dusk. The most immediate out-come from the meeting, aside from growing friendships, was that one of the men chose to have installed security cameras, motion sensitive, at the front and side doors, the vestry, the office, and the rectory. And by the first of the next month, the rectory had a full compliment, as Frs. Kent and Len moved back in.

The 10:00 o'clock Mass began with the sanctuary half full, an attendance double what had been there the preceding Sunday. Father Len was the liturgist. Everything was going as planned until after the Epistle reading. Then he began a five minute unplanned, and uninvited announcement of who was in the hospital, or nursing home care center, who was on the Compassion Committee's list, and who had requested prayers.

"What's this all about?" Mike wondered to himself

Finally Fr Len got around to the Gospel reading and asked everyone to stand, after he gave another impromptu lengthy introduction to the homily series, The Greatest Stories Ever Told.

"My gosh! Where is he going with this?" Mike pondered as he watched the well planned mass going into a death spin.

"The reading is from the Gospel of St. Luke, the fifteenth chapter, Fr. Len intoned. "It is a triplet of the same message. You will recall the first parable is that of a shepherd who had ninety nine sheep safely resting, and one who had strayed. When the shepherd searched and found his lost sheep, he returned it to the sheepfold, saying to those nearby, 'Rejoice with me, for that which was lost is found.' The second parable is that of a woman who lost a silver coin in her house, and swept and searched the house until the coin was found, She cried to her neighbors, 'rejoice with me for that which was lost is found!'

"I can't believe he is doing this!" Mike watched the time slip away.

Finally, Fr. Len said, "Now listen to St. Luke's message for us today. I'm reading from the 15th chapter, verses 11 through 32." He read the lesson, and Mike wondered how many other services he had sabotaged with his unsolicited remarks.

Mike stood in the pulpit, looking at the congregation. His notes were before him, but he gazed a moment longer, then asked them to pray. As he began the homily he didn't even look at his notes. He reminded them of the pictures on their milk carton showing missing children. "Over a million children are either abducted or run away each year in our nation. Only a third of them are ever returned home. With that as the framework, as Fr. McDonald has eloquently explained, let's examine

# THE CORRUPTION OF FATHER MIKE

the very familiar story. We may know the surface facts, but the depths of the story can touch our lives in an amazing and awesome way." The outline of his homily was: 1.)setting; 2.) the nature of sin is an affront to God; 3.)certain judgment; 4.) forgiveness and ultimate reconciliation.

Sixteen minutes later, he concluded the homily saying, "The father still tried to get his son to come in and join the celebration. 'Son, you are always with me, and all that is mine is yours.' That is so difficult for the elder brother to believe. It is hard for us to believe. God is saying to us this morning, 'All that is mine is yours.' The father goes on to say, 'it is fitting to make merry and be glad, for this your brother was dead and is alive; he was lost and is found.' At this point the curtain falls. We don't know what happened. Does the elder brother remain in the darkness and the cold, with his bitterness and resentment; or will he enter into the father's house and celebration?"

Mike had not taken his eyes off the congregation, looking intently from face to face. "This is the question we must decide. Some of us are lost in the far country. Some of us are in the depths of despair of separation from God because of some consequence of following an illusion about the joy to be found in the far country. Perhaps some of us are like the elder brother. We really resent the graciousness of God The other day I saw a picture of a little boy's face on my milk carton. My attention was captured by the word MISSING! Above the picture of this child with large searching eyes was a phone number of an organization that wants to help."

"I wonder this morning if we care about those missing – those who are lost? Are you willing to be the kind of community of faith that cares about those who are lost or hurt? Perhaps it seems terribly old fashioned to talk about having a burden of concern for the lost. I don't think it is old fashioned at all. I think the pictures on the milk cartons reminds us that we are still living in a world where if we don't care about the lost, they will never be found. We have great news to share about a God who is waiting to receive those who will return to him – a God who will take even the burden of the cross, shedding the blood not of a sacrificial animal, but giving his own life in Christ Jesus to demonstrate once and for all the depth of his commitment to offer us total forgiveness and acceptance. What a joy it is to know and receive that glorious relationship. We have a Lord who says to us, 'Rejoice with me, for he is found!' That is part of our mission and privilege today. Pray with me."

Most of those present were not even aware that the mass had run a bit later than most, but all were aware of the courage and dedication of their new priest. It was indeed a new beginning at Blessed Sacraments.

That evening as the Young Adult Fellowship was meeting in the church parlor, the coffee and cookies were just served when Fr. McDonald was surprised to see Fr. O'Malley come through the door with a large grin. "Good evening Father," he greeted.

"Good evening to you all," Mike answered, "I was just in the building and wanted to have a chance to say 'hello.' Fellowship is such an important part of our life here at Blessed Sacrament. Don't you love the thought of fellowship? You know the Greek word for it is 'Koinonia.'" Looking briefly at Fr. McDonald, he asked, "Could I just share this briefly?" He produced a small

# THE CORRUPTION OF FATHER MIKE

Bible, and turned to a bookmarked page, then read Acts 2: 42 – 47. "In this passage," he began, "we have a kind of lightning summary of the characteristics of the early church, which was a learning church." He explained that the word "doctrine" was not passive, but active. "It was a church of fellowship." Then he explained the concept of togetherness as a band of brothers who a.) prayed together; b.) were reverent, like one who is awed by the greatness of the temple of the living God; c.) were a band where things happened, where signs and miraculous events occurred, and heroic deeds were attempted for God; d.) the brothers shared an intense feeling of responsibility for each other. A real Christian could not bear to have too much when others have too little; e.) It was a worshipping church, for the brothers never forgot to visit God's house; and f.) It was a happy church that others could not help but like. There were two Greek words for good. One is 'agathos' which simply describes a thing as good. The other is 'kalos' which means a thing is not only good, but it has a goodly appearance, an attractiveness. There are some people that we might call iceberg Christians. They go through the motions of loyalty, but most of their lives are hidden, distant, unavailable. You could never go weep your heart out on their shoulder." He shared a cookie with the group, then thanked them for allowing him to barge in upon them.

 A little after ten, when Len returned to the rectory, he found Mike sitting in the parlor, waiting for him. "Cup of tea?" Mike asked. When Len was seated, Mike said softly. "If you ever again forget the boundaries of responsibilities, and presume that my efforts need your assistance, I will publicly embarrass you. Tonight I embarrassed myself to remind you that our responsibilities are definite, and important. If you cannot respect that for our staff's unity, at least respect it for yourself."

"Father O'Malley, I had no intent to insult you or the office you hold, I simply wanted to ease any anxiety you might be feeling, " Len said softly.

Just as softly, Mike said, "I wasn't feeling any anxiety until you decided to make a six minute report of the walking wounded, and then went rogue free-style Bible-scholar on me. I want you to know that if God and I are not adequate for the task, we sure as hell don't need you to fix it. If your tasks are not satisfying enough we can fix that. Tonight I need you to understand that I am not Fr. Michaels, and will not allow you to interfere with my duties as they have been explained to me by the Bishop."

Len looked at the batons hanging outside the bedroom door and realized that he had underestimated, or misunderstood the depth of this young man, and a wave of appreciation gave him goose-bumps. "I pledge you that it won't happen again. But I want you to know there was no embarrassment for you this evening. The group was delighted that you dropped in, and commented that the interest of the senior priest was a unique treat. Your remarks, which I fully understood, was the catalyst of some spirited conversation. They hope you will visit again, soon."

There was no more confusion about leadership. The three priests remembered their duties well. Mike remembered again to pay the business tax on the interest income from the savings account. Attendance grew through Lent, and when Mike invited the acolytes to assist in a moving Maundy Thursday communion candle lighting, folks were talking about the replacement of the pews that were in storage. Easter was a marvelous full-house celebration, just like the "old days."

In June, Mike introduced to the congregation the opportunity of a Sunday evening Folk Vespers service, led by a group from the University. "'Vespers'", Mike explained, "is Latin for 'prayers,' which may be said or sung together. The group call themselves, 'Primin' the Pump'. Their signature song is 'Primin' the pump of the livin' water, keep primin' the pump don't let the well run dry. Keep primin' the pump of the livin' water, don't let the spirit die.'" The first evening there was only a handful of Blessed Sacrament members and well over a hundred students in attendance. By mid July the service was standing-room only, and the Oregonian sent a reporter to do an article on the rejuvenation of a downtown church. It was welcome news to the folks in the community who longed for the sound of Blue-grass harmony and the rhythm of the strumming guitars. It was also welcome to the rhythm of a dark element with criminal intent. They were about to collide.

The 3rd of August was a warm evening. Mike and the church treasurer stood outside reflecting on the abrupt turnaround in the congregation. The treasurer said, "We are shocked, Fr. Mike. We all thought this would be a terrible drain on the budget, and it is way beyond covering the expenses. I think we can start talking about giving to missions again." His hand rested fondly on Mike's shoulder.

"It is working better than we hoped," Mike reflected. "Tonight I received another dozen cards of folks who are interested in membership here . That should put a wide smile on Fr. Len's face." They parted, allowing Mike to make his way to the rectory next door.

It was almost midnight when Mike heard a girl's soft voice say, "Yoo-hoo, Mr. Priest." Quickly Mike pulled on a bathrobe and made his way to the parlor, picking up his baton on the way. He held it behind his leg, ready for action if needed. Turning on a light he was amazed to find a lovely woman in the process of disrobing! She didn't say another word just stepped out of her skirt and slip, then unbuttoned her blouse and dropped it too. She was pulling a bra strap off her shoulder when Mike said, "Stop that! Have you been drinking?" For once he was sorry that with three living together, the priests had fallen into the casual habit of leaving an unlocked front door. She stepped toward him, and Mike said, "You must stop this now." She seemed to stumble to her knees as she pulled the strap free, exposing a bare breast. Before Mike could react, she grasped his leg, and pulled the robe away from it. A flash of a camera was warning that she was not alone.

"Oh that's a good one, Lee. Can you push in a little tighter?" Another camera flash as Mike gave a powerful kick, sending the woman across the room. "Hey Jack," the angry photographer blurted. "Move another inch and I will shoot you with more than this fucking camera. Are you alright, Lee?" he asked the woman as she stood up, replacing her bra.

"Whatever you have in mind is a bad idea," Mike said softly. "My advice is that you pick up your trash and leave." He stood statue still, but had one foot behind him as a brace.

"Shut your pious face, Mr. Holiness, or I'll put your lights out!' The man took a couple steps toward Mike. It was then that Lee noticed the baton. "He has a night stick!" she warned. The man hesitated. Their purpose was extortion, not armed conflict. This mark couldn't pay up if he was dead. Stepping back he said, "Well Mr. Vet-ran, I think she just saved your ass." The use of that name clarified Mike's memory; he knew the identity of the cameraman. Lee said, "I think this must be the one who banged up Captain Robert's kid. Let's go!" But her level gaze into Mike's eyes had reminded him of her beauty, and identity too. She was Leanne Levine; and he was Lt. Sam French of the Portland Police.

As the man was backing toward the door, he said "I'll be back next Sunday night to pick up a thousand bucks cash for these pictures, or the Bishop and the newspaper will have some shocking headlines."

Only when the door was closed and locked did Frs. Kent and Len appear. They had heard most if not all of what was said, and were both upset. "This is terrible," Kent moaned. "What will the Bishop think?" Len was equally concerned but wondered how the Pastoral Committee would take the news. Mike thought they both were worried about administration, and had not thought about being concerned for their colleague.

"I'll make a phone call in the morning, and if Claire has remembered to put fresh tapes in the security system, I will miss our staff get-together. I'm sure the Prosecuting Attorney's office will want to see it as soon as possible. I already know the identity of our visitors. Gentlemen, let's do two things. Let's pray for our enemies that this problem might find a gentle and wholesome conclusion; and let's remember to lock the damned door when we are the last one in. O.K.?"

Just after breakfast Mike called the prosecuting attorney's office, asking for Brad Phillips. When his happy voice answered he said, "...but my rate has gone up from $25 dollars an hour."

"Mine has too," his good friend responded.

"Hey, I saw that you have been posted to Blessed Sacrament! What a promotion, I think" Brad was busy, but not to the extent of trying to shorten the call. "What can I do for you, father?" he asked.

"This morning I think I get to pay back a great big favor you did for me. I remember that you were eager to get some evidence on Leanne Levine. Do you still want it?" he asked almost playfully. "And with it comes evidence of a very dirty cop."

"You've got proof?" Brad nearly whispered.

"I've got them on our security tape, and the other two priests heard them try to shake me down last night. Yeah, we've got proof."

Brad was so eager to get the tape that he drove the four blocks from his office to pick it up. When he viewed it, he agreed that this was going to be a very big deal.

"Lt. French has been on several complaint lists, but this is the first time we have hard evidence. He seemed to have come into a lot of money that can't be explained. Maybe this is how he came by it. I will swear out a warrant for his arrest as soon as I can get back to the office." Now he was in a big hurry. Leanne was arrested at her home, and Lt. French was arrested when he reported for his shift. It was indeed headline stuff, and Mike was glad not to be part of it.

Brad took depositions from Mike, Kent and Len; then he interviewed Leanne, which gave him the opportunity to offer her the advantage of turning state's evidence on Mr. French. She knew about the train "accident" insurance fraud, and the school bus. She had been "persuaded" by her dad to be involved. There were almost thirty names on her list of prominent

# THE CORRUPTION OF FATHER MIKE

citizens placed in compromised situations leading to extortion of one kind or another; two judges and four attorneys were on the list. Finally she was charged with lewd behavior and extortion. She pleaded "guilty" to the charges rather than risk a longer sentence with a trial. She was out on bail until the judge's sentencing hearing. Mr. French was denied bail until his trial date in September.

Mike received a letter that had been forwarded from his University box address. It was from former Sergeant John White. Mike read it immediately. It had been a long while since they had heard from one another. He was happy to be out. His dad needed him at home in Oklahoma. His dad's construction business was about shot; there's just not enough demand for new houses. Fr. Blake had given him the good news about Mike's schooling. The chaplain had been a source of information and inspiration until a new assignment as security in the Philippines had broken the contact. Now discharged, he had a lady friend, but needed some advice. John closed by asking if Mike would have some time for him if he drove out to Portland. There was an immediate and positive response.

The Sunday after Labor Day was especially busy. Children were back in school, new programs were beginning. The fresh attendance growth seemed to be showing up all at once. Even the balcony had to be opened to hold them all. Fr. Len was leading the service happily. He could scarcely believe the growth in only eight months. The Psalter for the morning was the 51st Psalm. He read the familiar words, then sat down, eager for Fr. Mike's homily.

After a very brief prayer the priest began: "David the king was in big trouble – and he knew it! Bathsheba was pregnant .

He was the father of the child. Her husband Uriah was serving as a soldier in the king's army at the battle front. He was a pagan convert to Judaism and one of the most valiant and courageous men in all Israel. To hide his sin of adultery, David sent a letter to the commander of the army to allow Uriah to return home to visit his wife. David was thinking, of course, that an intimate visit with Bathsheba would erase any suspicion of her infidelity and David's involvement. But Uriah did an amazing thing. He didn't take advantage of the luxury availed to him saying that while his fellow soldiers were in battle he could not be in such comfort. I'm sure that David was stunned by this kind of fidelity and commitment. Here indeed is an amazing picture – soldier, a pagan convert to the faith – is revealed as more moral than David, the giant killer, the man of faith."

"The plot thickens as David invites Uriah to the palace for dinner; he deliberately tries to get Uriah intoxicated, thinking he would then go home and once again create doubt as to the fatherhood of Bathsheba's pregnancy. Once again Uriah foils the plan by not going home but remains in the king's palace. Finally in frustration, David writes a letter to Joab, the commander, and delivered by none other than Uriah, telling Joab to place Uriah in the most fierce fighting, and then to draw back from him that he may be struck down and die. Isn't it ironic that Uriah would be asked to carry the letter containing his own death sentence from the king whom he trusted to his commanding officer whom he respected? Such is the depth of treachery of the cover-up, which sin and evil began to generate."

"The story of 2 Samuel concludes with these words: 'When the wife of Uriah heard that Uriah her husband was dead, she made lamentations for her husband. And when the mourning was over, David sent and brought her to his house, and she became his wife, and bore him a son. But the thing that David had done displeased the Lord. And the Lord sent Nathan to David.' You get the distinct impression from the text that the lamentations and mourning was shallow and insincere – that Bathsheba was somehow involved in the conspiracy."

"You remember how Nathan, the prophet, walked into the palace and began to tell a story to the king, 'There were two men in a certain city, the one rich and the other quite poor. The rich man had very many flocks and herds; but the poor man had nothing but one little ewe lamb, which he had bought. And he brought it up, and it grew up with him and his children; it used to eat of his morsel, and drink from his cup, and lie in his bosom, and it was like a daughter to him. Now there came a traveler to the rich man, and he was unwilling to take one of his own flock or herd to prepare for the wayfarer who had come to him, but he took the poor man's lamb, and prepared it for the man who had come to him. When David heard the story he was furious with anger. He shouted in a voice that must have echoed through the palace, 'As the Lord lives, the man who has done this deserves to die!'"

"Nathan then looked at David and spoke slowly, 'You are the man. Thus says the Lord, the God of Israel, 'I anointed you king over Israel; I delivered you out of the hand of Saul, and I gave you the master's house, and your master's wives into your bosom, and gave you the house of Israel and Judah; and if this were too little, I would add to you as much more. Why have you despised the word of the Lord, to do what is evil in his sight? You have smitten Uriah the Hittite with the sword, and have taken his wife to be your wife, and have slain him with the sword of the Ammonites. Now therefore the sword shall never depart from your house...'"

"David cried out, 'I have sinned against the Lord!'"

"David's halo had slipped! He was no longer the innocent son of Jesse, the simple shepherd boy. He was no longer the courageous youth who had faced the giant Goliath. He was no longer the hero of the people – the king without flaw or fault. Now the truth was known – and would be forever known. He was David the adulterer. He was David the murderer, the liar, the deceiver, the killer of a trusted husband and soldier who believed in his integrity. He was the coward who tried to cover his guilt in a devious scheme. It was a devastating moment, not only for David, but for all Israel."

"The fifty first Psalm was David's cry – his prayer for forgiveness when he knew that he finally had to face reality. He was confronted with the reality of what he had done. He was faced with the inescapable fact of his own sin – the crisis of his own moral failure. Today's lesson helps us deal with the crisis of guilt and of moral failure. What do we do, when we know that we have sinned and fallen short. What do we do when our halo has slipped? "

"I can tell you that first of all we can refuse to trivialize our sin with the shrug of the shoulders and up turned palms. That's what David tried to do at first. He was trivializing the matter when he sent the message to Joab saying, ' Do not let the matter trouble you, for the sword devours now one and now another...' We trivialize when we say, what does it really matter? Everyone else is doing it too. Everyone tells little lies. Everyone cheats now and then. Every one breaks the laws some. I heard about a man who sent the IRS a check along with a letter of explanation that said, 'Gentlemen: Enclosed you will find a check for $150. I cheated on my tax return last year, and I haven't been able to sleep ever since. If I still can't sleep, I'll send you the rest.' Trivializing doesn't work! Not with God. Sin is not trivial. Not for David – not for us."

"Secondly, we can refuse to project. Through projection we start to see in others the sins and faults we do not like in ourselves. I have at times found myself becoming critical of other priests. However when I looked more closely at it, I have been shocked to discover that criticism is something that really irritates me in other people. It is something I don't like about myself. My mother tells me that when I was very young – when I would break something, spill something or make a big mess, I would go to her and take her hand, then lead her to the mess, or the broken pieces. I'd point to her and ask, 'Who did that?' as if to imply that I was totally innocent. After all, I wouldn't be reporting a crime that I had committed, would I? It must have been someone else. David was projecting as he became angry and shouted, 'As the Lord lives, that man who has done this deserves to die.' We can refuse to trivialize, rationalize or project."

"But what we can do is individualize. That was the real turning point for David. It was a major step forward when he finally said, 'I have sinned against the lord. That is such a hard step for many of us to take. He said..'Against thee, thee only have I sinned and done that which is evil in thy sight...' David suddenly was faced with the realization that his sin was not against Bathsheba or Uriah, Joab or the valiant soldiers, it was primarily against God. In committing adultery with

Bathsheba, in killing Uriah, in commanding the soldiers to act in treachery, he had really sinned against God. That was an important step for David to take. It is interesting that God did not send a priest to describe for David the atonement process or the appropriate ritual sacrifice. He did not send a rabbi to teach him doctrine or theology. He sent a prophet to tell a story that would enable David to individualize and identify the reality of the impact of his own sin. That is a very painful but necessary step. We make it personal."

"One of the most elegant voices for peace in our time is that of a little ten year old girl named Samantha Smith. She suggested that the President of the United States should send his granddaughter to live in Russia, and that the President of Russia should send his granddaughter to live in the United States. She said that no leader would drop a bomb on a country where his granddaughter is living. She suggested that the countries exchange children and young people so they would get to know one another on a personal and individual basis. She's right; we must not think of faceless enemies. We must understand that we are talking about people – Christian people – many of them are children, young adults, babies, grandparents, who have the same dreams and hopes and wishes that we do. We must learn to individualize."

"When we begin to do that we finally understand that is how God deals with the sins we have committed, individually. There is someone in this very room who is terrified their sins will be revealed, another who is certain their dearest relationship is destroyed, another who has given up all hope of ever feeling acceptable again. When we begin to stand with David, we know there is also in this very room a God who stretches

# THE CORRUPTION OF FATHER MIKE

out loving arms to rescue and redeem us. When we claim our rightful role in the world, the church will be the exciting place where we are learning to respond to the needs of those hurting people one step, one person at a time." The sanctuary was breathless still.

"There is one more big step: we can ask for and receive God's forgiveness and grace. Do you recall the words that opened the Psalm? 'Have mercy on me, O God, according to your steadfast love, according to your abundant mercy blot out my transgressions.'

David understands what is difficult for many of us. The focus must be on God, and not on us. God loves you, has always, and will forever love you. Nothing you have ever done can make God stop loving you. It is all about a holy and righteous loving God. So David turns to him in prayer. There follows one of the greatest prayers of scripture: 'Create in me a clean heart O God, and put a new and right spirit within me. Cast me not away from thy presence, and take not thy Holy Spirit from me. Restore to me the joy of thy salvation and uphold me with a willing spirit.' My friends, that is the gift God has for you today. It is the gift of the joy of his salvation."

"Then, and only then, does David speak of changed behavior, of doing something with his life because God has given him a new heart, a fresh start. David vows, 'Then I will teach transgressors thy ways, and sinners will return to thee.' David goes on to say 'O Lord, open thou my lips, and my mouth shall show forth thy praise. For thou hast no delight in sacrifice; were I to give a burnt offering, thou wouldst not be pleased. The sacrifice acceptable to God is a broken spirit, a broken and contrite heart, O God, thou wilt not despise.'"

"Many years ago David put a loyal young soldier in the lead of an attack against an Ammonite city. At the given signal all of his battle brothers abandoned him. He was left absolutely alone. In that moment when he looked around and saw himself stranded, standing there alone facing an attacking army, he must have realized the treachery, as he watched his friends draw away. Perhaps that is how you feel this morning. Perhaps you feel abandoned or forsaken. Perhaps you feel overwhelmed with problems, and the adversity of life. There is one who is called the Son of David, who will never abandon you! He is with you right now. In his hands is the print of the nails. In his side the sign of the spear, on his head the crown of thorns. He has already won the victory. He takes you by the hand and leads you forward through the forces that seem to be overwhelming you. He will lead you to victory. Trust in him. There is forgiveness for every past sin. There is a chance to start again with a clean heart. There is grace that can purge us so that in spite of everything, we can know the joy and certainty of his salvation. I urge you this morning to accept that relationship – that gift of grace and peace right now. What are the words of the old gospel hymn? 'He breaks the power of cancelled sin, He sets the prisoner free; His blood can make the foulest clean, His blood availed for me.'"

Fr. Len announced the offering, and prepared the new communion trays that would be passed through the large crowd. Then he prayed the prayer of consecration, and the servers began to distribute the bread and wine.

Fr. Mike spoke softly the words of distribution as he watched the trays being passed from person to person: "Be assured of this: God loves you; God forgives you; God has a holy plan for you, and even now equips you with faith." – "Hear this good news: Jesus forgives the past, empowers the present, and gives hope to the future." – "The past never has the last word; the powers of evil will never write the final chapters of history; thanks be to God, who gives us the victory through our Lord, Jesus the Christ." "There is hope for us even in our failures. By God's Word we are cleansed, and in God's Spirit we are made strong."

A song was shared and Fr. Mike gave his favorite benediction: "As you leave this place you can go in confidence, for you know whose love sustains you, and whose Holy Hand guides you until we meet again. Amen" In the balcony there was one who wept quietly. She had never experienced such honest love, such powerful acceptance.

Fr. Mike was standing in the narthex near the front doors, bidding folks a blessing on their way home. He made sure there was ample space for those who wanted to simply leave, but so many wanted to applaud the changes at Blessed Sacrament. Several of the folks from the University were in attendance, to his surprise. Even Fr. Lopez was there saying that the sermon was even more outstanding than the scholarship that prepared it. Mike smiled widely at that compliment. One of the church Trustees shook Mike's hand saying, "I suppose we are going to need more parking spaces." His tone of voice erased the smile. Fr. Mike thanked Mr. Kellogg for once again pointing out a challenge. Finally the crowd began to thin out, several small clumps of conversations lingering. And then he saw her, standing near the far wall examining a stained glass. He walked over and said, "Leanne, I'm so glad to see you here. I have wondered about your court date."

Her smile was fragile, but sincere. "You remember my name; thank you, But then I guess after our call on the rectory, you couldn't forget."

"Actually, I have remembered you since we met at Legacy. I was the intake processor who first interviewed you. You sure had me fooled." His warm smile told her there were no hard feelings.

"I remember that you treated me nice. Most men who think they are dealing with a young drunken prostitute are not so nice at all. You stood out as someone who really saw me, and didn't blow the whistle on my lies."

Mike said with even more warmth, "I'm not all that noble. I believed you were seventeen, and living with you grandparents. I was pretty sure you were not guilty of the other stuff."

"I'm glad I came here today. I wasn't sure if I would be welcome. This feels wonderful. My sentencing hearing will be Wednesday, and I'll learn how much time I get. I wanted to tell you that the Prosecuting Attorney has made it real clear to my dad that if anything happens to you because I am going to prison, extra time will be added to my sentence, so take care of yourself." There was that perky spark that made her unforgettable. "I also want to know if I could send you a note every now and then? I joke about it, but I have been too beat up by my dad to want to stay in touch with him, and I don't have anyone else." Her voice trailed away weakly.

"I'll be glad to hear from you and will write back, I promise. You know, if you think about it, your time in a corrections facility might be a good time to finish up your schooling." It was a positive way Mike could end their conversation.

"Ha, what schooling? I really wanted to go to Corvallis to

become an accountant, but dad had other plans for my life. I just want to feel clean again."

"I see you have one of our worship folders; that has contact information for the church and a 24 hour number at the rectory. Write to me with your mailing address." He had the notion that she would stay and talk as long as he would. "Thanks again for visiting us." When she shook his hand he was struck by how small it was, how soft it was and how it warmed his heart. She was struck by how strong his hand felt, yet how gently he held hers, and how it warmed her heart.

On Wednesday night, just as Mike was brushing his teeth getting ready for bed, the phone rang. His first thought was some medical emergency in the parish, which Fr. Kent upstairs, could handle. "Good evening, this is Fr. Mike." There was a long pause on the line; then he heard Leanne's voice say simply, "The Judge gave me forty months, with time off for good behavior." Another long pause followed.

"Well it's good that the wondering is over. Did you expect a shorter sentence?"

"My fears were that it might be longer, and my hope was probation, which certainly didn't happen." Her voice was small almost like a child.

"O.K. Kiddo," Mike said as warmly as he could, "I remember in class that we were told that the best way to deal with negative energy is not to fight against it. Instead make positive use of that energy by redirecting it into something constructive. By simply focusing the energy of your frustration on a worthwhile goal you can make it work to your advantage. You will probably see some pretty angry folks who spend day after day feeling rotten. But I am sure of this, each instance of negative energy has a positive counterpart. There will also be folks around you who are friendly and even helpful if you are open to their guidance. You will have just as much time to study as any Oregon State student. The same study material will be available; it's going to be up to you."

"That sounds real nice, but I'm a little slow to accept advice from someone who has it so good." Her tone of voice was not aggressive, as it could have been.

"You mean me?" he asked, "The truth is, some really bad things did happen to me in Korea. I came home with terrible memories, and only about twenty percent hearing in my good ear. I could have sat back on disability but I gave myself to school, because there are people who cared and would pitch in."

"I can't imagine you as disabled. I'm sorry to imply... Your opinion of me is really important. I did some very bad things for my dad, but none of the things most people think of. I deserve to be in OCI, but you made me feel like I also belonged in church. I haven't been in church much, but I have never imagined that it could be as good as last Sunday. Do you really think I can find something good in lock-up?"

"Yes I do. I think every moment is a chance to make your best choice in the circumstances. Every difficult decision serves as an opportunity to take a step up and show your deeply held dreams. You can do this! If you see it as a great opportunity, it will be just that." Mike would have said a little more, but Leanne interrupted him.

"I'm going to try really hard, and if you are feeding me a line, I'm going to be very, very disappointed."

"Kiddo, if you try even a little, you will be a superstar of accomplishment in however many months you are there. In the morning, when you are given that pair of coveralls, wear it just as if it was a matching skirt and sweater of a freshman at OSC. You will feel great, and you will be great." He was convincing himself, if not her.

She said, "Thanks a lot for this pep talk. I was a bit bummed out. You helped a lot. Goodnight; I'll write you with good news."

She did. In the Monday mail was an envelope with a Department of Corrections return address. It caused a bit of stir in the office, until Fr. Mike explained that he was assigned as a care custodian to the inmate that had tried the extortion attempt in the rectory. It was not quite true, but convincing enough to quiet their curiosity. When he opened Leanne's letter it was almost like talking with her: "Good morning, Father Mike. You were right; this is not as bad as I thought it was going to be. The staff is cordial if I am first, which is fun. It lets me choose what sort of day I'm going to have. Hey, isn't that what you said? I was given a choice the first day I was here, to choose a job or school. Just like you said. I chose school and I have two work books already. The woman in charge of the education stuff is only a tiny bit older than me, but just between you and me, she weighs at least three times what I do. You were right. There are some real angry women in here, but at least as many that I would call friendly. I'm going to do O.K. I hope to hear from you. Your friend, Leanne"

September was a very hectic month with new programs, greater attendance and more income than the church was accustomed to. The Trustees saw it as a windfall time and developed a laundry list of repair projects that had been waiting. The most dramatic was their desire to switch the furnace system from the crude oil boiler to a new natural gas forced air.

# The Plot Thickens

~~~❖~~~

As Fr. Mike was passing through the office, Claire asked, "Father, you keep getting these General Service Administration brochures. I was about to toss this one. Would you like me to get your name off the list? And you have two Dept of Correction letters today."

It had been a while since Mike had given a thought to John Rice and the folks at St. Joseph. He took the folder from her saying, "Not just yet, it reminds me of the former parish, and I like it." He dropped it on his desk, thinking he would probably throw it away later. But on the back were listed properties that would be auctioned off as surplus in October, two of which were sizeable enough to catch and hold his attention. They were just west of Burlington, about ten miles away.

There was a Trustees breakfast the next day, followed by a staff meeting. When those tasks were completed, Mike drove out Highway 30. He found a lot of empty property, and not knowing the size of what he saw, he was ready to call it quits. Just west of the marina, however, he noticed a large plot that had been used to dump rocks and dirt, stumps and logs from clearing and widening the road. If he were to guess, that is the sort of government property that would be surplus. It was fairly wide, from the highway out to the Willamette River, flat with only low brush. It was easy to drive by and see nothing of interest.

On the way back to the church, Mike thought, "But it is a great place to build something of interest."

He called Brad Phillips immediately."Brad, I need a couple more hours of your time." "Yeah at the new rate." "My eccentric friend would love to bid on some GSA property that will be auctioned off the 8th of October. Can you represent him?" "Yeah, items C1163, which is 245 acres, and C1162, which is 370 acres." "That's right. It is a lot of ground. I think he is doing this as a test, you know like a fleece." "If you can get the first one under twenty five thousand, and the second one for the same…." "That's right, they are two parcels which run together. He said there is a nice bonus in it for you." "I don't know I'm only telling you what he said." "Yes, he will pay your hourly rate regardless of your auction prowess." "No, I don't have a clue what he wants with all that space. But knowing him, I think it will be interesting." "Yeah, I will bring a cashier's check for a ten thousand dollar down payment, balance within three business days." "I don't know. Could you use 'in care of you at your office address?'" "Yes, he'll pay a retainer."

Mike realized he had to be careful with this sort of thinking. It was getting him pumped full of adrenaline; he was so distracted he couldn't take care of his real duties. He had developed a habit of putting off answering Leanne's letters until after supper. It was less of a distraction then, and a pleasant way to end the day; he had a ton of great quotes to send along to her.

"Hello Leanne, I'm glad to hear that you are making progress, and I can sure identify with the feeling you are having about school. Sometimes when things fail to go the way you planned, they turn out even better than you could have possibly expected. I think there is an art to welcome life's surprises, and choose to see the positive value that is in each one of them. Don't be too quick to place judgments on the people, situations or events in your life. In everything that comes along, there is an opportunity for you to more fully discover and express your true purpose. This moment is filled with magnificent possibilities, and this moment is when you can bring the best of them to life. Let go of those burdens you really don't need, and welcome the beauty of now! I hope that doesn't sound preachy. Good night. Blessings, Fr. Mike."

It was easy with so many daily and weekly responsibilities to lose track of time as it sped by. Mike was surprised when Brad called to say he had good news. "There were four or five of us bidding on the first parcel. I heard someone comment that it had utilities available, but the second one did not. Three of the bidders dropped out pretty early. The guy that was bidding against me thought his twenty thousand would take it. When I raised him two more, he folded like a wet tent. No one bid on the second parcel so I got it for openers, ten thousand. The balance due after the down payment was made is twenty two thousand with transfer fees of two hundred nine dollars. Do you think your eccentric millionaire will be happy?"

"I think he will turn cartwheels!" Mike nearly giggled. "It's still a mystery what all that land will be used for. I just hope it isn't too extreme. By the way have you seen the new Buick? Which do you like better - that or a ninety eight Oldsmobile?"

"Are you kidding. I'm still on the bottom of the pile around here, and Connie is pregnant. I can't even look at a used car."

"Hey, congratulations dad," Mike said genuinely happy. "If you're going to have a family would you prefer a station wagon?"

"Knock it off, or I'll come over there and tie you in a knot.

I'm not joking anymore."

"Neither am I," Mike said warmly. "I'll see you in the next couple days when I get all this silly stuff wrapped up."

By the time Mike had cashier's checks for the land and for Olson Buick, who promised to give Brad a choice of either a new sedan Royal or a station wagon, there was still a larger balance than the original deposit for Venite Village.

The first hiccup with Blessed Sacrament occurred at a Saturday wine and cheese forum. After a very jovial beginning, a cynic opened a very tender subject. "Father O'Malley, a number of us are upset with this affair you have going with the penitentiary woman." The packed room was suddenly uncomfortably silent.

"Ray," the priest said gently, "I don't think this is the sort of thing we intended these conversations to handle."

"It is the biblical way," the abrasive man began. "I'm supposed to bring it before the elders when I have a complaint against another."

"To be accurate, Ray, I think the process outlined is you should approach the one who offends you first; then if resolution is not found prayerfully, take it to two elders, not two dozen. You have publicly struck a sensitive and inflammatory subject. What are you and a number of others upset about?" Obviously Fr. Mike was not too concerned about the subject.

"You have been seen mailing love letters almost every day, and receiving them from her, to the detriment of your duties." His face and neck were turning pink with emotion.

"Ray, would you believe that I send one note of encouragement to Miss Levine a week, and I write it in the evening when all my other tasks are complete?"

# THE CORRUPTION OF FATHER MIKE

"No, I won't believe that," he said as he lost control of more emotion. "I won't believe anything from a person who has lied to the secretary, and sneaked down to Salem twice this week." Now several of the folks were becoming visibly uncomfortable.

"Mr. Kellogg, this has gone way beyond what is reasonable. I have never lied to Claire, and I have never driven the car more than ten miles from the church. I think further discussion of this should happen with the Pastoral Committee. Please, out of respect for your friends if not yourself, let's change the subject."

"Yeah, sneak away to the committee," the out of control man fumed. "Nothing like this ever happened when Fr. Michaels was here."

Gently Fr. Mike asked, "Do you miss him?"

"Damn right I miss him! We all do! The whole church is sick over the changes that have happened this year." Now that it was said, he sat up a bit more forward.

"Mr. Kellogg, are you willing to test the validity of that right here with these friends?"

"Yeah of course I am; you'll see" But his arms folded over his chest as a sign of defense.

"Friends, you will not hurt my feelings with an honest vote. Do you agree with Mr. Kellogg? Raise your hands if you do." Not one single hand was raised, "I think we should have a time of prayer before we adjourn. It might be difficult to chat after such a serious accusation."

"Don't bother," the angry man stood up, "and don't blame me for another screwed up program. I told you Fr. Michaels was the finest priest this church has ever had." He closed the door loudly behind him.

Mike shook his head. "What I am most afraid of is one gossip, spreading a groundless rumor, can destroy all the gain we have enjoyed this year. As God is my witness, there is not a speck of romance in any of the notes exchanged with a young woman who is frightened and lonely. She came to our church seeking wholesome friends and does not deserve anything less. I still have a need for prayer. They all bowed. "God our Heavenly Father, you are a God of peace. Help us to make peace in all our relationships with others. Give us the forbearing and the forgiving spirit that refuses to build walls between us and others. Keep us from being quick to take offence. Control both our temper and our tongue. Help us not be so quick to condemn what we do not understand, and when people think differently from us, help us to respect them, and the right to their opinions. Most of all, Lord, help us always treat others as we would have them treat us, in Jesus' precious name."

As the people filed out of the rectory, there was unanimous support and praise for the marvelous work Fr. Mike had accomplished. Mike prepared to retire for the evening, but the group who had witnessed Mr. Kellogg's crude behavior was on a phone campaign to neutralize or prevent a rumor storm, sharing the account of Ray's unmerited assault on the priest's honor.

The second Sunday of December the sanctuary was wonderfully decorated with evergreen swags and lights; the vocal group from Vespers was singing, 'Kyrie eleison,' 'Lord have mercy' as the Mass began. Fr. Mike gazed at the full house, and knew that the conversation about adding another service hour was appropriate. From the second row he recognized a smiling face: Sergeant John White! He gave Mike a salute of sorts, and received one in return. Mike had to remind himself to stay focused on the worship instead of memories of Korea. But when the mass was complete, there was a time of reunion.

"This is Judy, the lady I have told you so much about," John said proudly The attractive woman with a wide smile first shook Mike's hand and then delivered a warm hug. "She has agreed to be Mrs. White as soon as we get the job picture settled." Oh there was so much to talk about and so much Mike couldn't tell, just yet. But he was forming a plan for the future.

"Yeah, dad's along to chaperone. You know he's a hard shell Baptist, and wouldn't think of letting me come to Portland with Judy alone." He shook his head. "Cryin' out loud, he thinks I'm still sixteen."

Judy asked, "Has it been six years since you two were together?"

"Actually, it has been eight years, and yet I can remember our time together like it was just yesterday. Say, would you like a tour of the city; maybe get some lunch while we catch up?"

"Sure, if we can pick up dad. His name is Jerry. He wouldn't be happy if we left him out."

"Oh, he is definitely not going to be left out. Didn't you tell me that he has a construction business, with some equipment?"

"Yeah, we have a medium size cat, and a track hoe, with a dump truck."

While they drove around the city, marveling at all the bridges, the construction going on, and the mild winter weather, a plan was continuing to hatch in Mike's agenda. Finally, after they had eaten and were sitting near a fireplace at the Chart House, Mike asked about their work schedule.

John replied, "It depends on who you ask. Pa says we have lots of work, just not now. I say we have two small scraps to finish and then it's a frozen winter. There must be a foot of snow that won't melt until March at least."

"The reason I ask," Mike said leaning in confidentially, "I have a guy in the church who just bought about 600 acres that needs the brush scraped off. I think he is taking bids for it right now."

John asked, "Is it flat or hilly? Does it have a lot of trees and rocks that will be removed? And how far from the highway is it? Those are some important things to know."

"Well I think it is pretty flat, and it runs right beside the river, so I'm guessing that the soil is mostly dirt and sand. Highway 30 runs along the whole south side, so it's easy access." He watched the ideas blooming in both men.

Jerry asked, "How long do we have to get the job done? Is it one of those 'I need it yesterday' things?"

"You know, this is just his first step; so I don't think there is a great rush. But it is eventually going to be full of houses."

"How many do you suppose?" John asked now fully into the idea.

"I think he said a couple hundred at least; some affordable places on one side, and nicer ones on the other. Beat's me. He doesn't even have a plot plan yet." Mike was enjoying the interplay, and watched as Judy was swept up in it too.

"Well, when can we start?" Jerry asked eagerly.

"As I said, I'm just an eavesdropper. I think he's taking bids right now."

"Maybe if we did a good job clearing," John mused, "we could bid on some of the other stuff, even building some of the homes." He looked at Judy and said, "We could get married."

"I've been calculating in my head, " Jerry said finally. "If we allow $200 for fuel moving the equipment, and $400 for fuel doing the job, and $12,000 labor, I think we can have it skinned clean in a week. Do you think, Johnny?"

"Yeah, if we don't hit any surprises. But it might be smart to say ten days, just in case. That way we can make sure it's a clean job, front and back."

"If I told you that twenty thousand would be the low bid easy, would you guys take it?" Mike whispered.

"Of course," Jerry said, also in a confidential voice. "That would be like found money, for sure."

"Yes, it would." Mike agreed. "Stop by the church about four tomorrow, and I'll have a check for half now and half when the job is complete." He held out his hand for Jerry to agree, and then John, for whom he was doubly grateful. "But gentlemen, we are in the Christmas season, and I'm sure he wouldn't care if you wait until January to begin. That might even permit a wedding before you return."

Judy came around the table to kneel beside Mike. She gave him a hug and a gentle kiss, saying, "Thank you; John said you were an amazing fellow. I'm not sure how all this worked out. But if you tell me that God's hand is in it, I will believe you for sure."

That evening, Fr. Mike wrote to Leanne: "I'm sorry it has been a difficult week for you. When that happens to me, I know that a really good week is coming soon. Whatever happens, there is always a way forward. Remember that as you welcome each new moment and each new development. Out of any circumstance, you can find a positive pathway. In any situation, there is the opportunity to create success and to experience fulfillment. Be unconditionally thankful for the moment you are in. Because the moment you're in is filled with real possibilities. Your gratitude will enable you to see the best of those possibilities. Your expectation of finding the best way forward will enable you to move toward it. I am proud of your progress. You are on the way to reach your goal! Blessings, Fr. Mike"

He had trouble sleeping. The thought that he had rushed into something, without carefully thinking it through nagged at him. But then he argued back, there is no plan, no schedule. He had simply opened a useful and very helpful opportunity. There was still one more step to be taken before serious decisions would present themselves. He must have a plan, a design, an architect's rendering of the whole concept, instead of random floating thoughts. Right after the staff meeting, he called the Department of Architecture at Portland State College. He asked the head of the department, "Would your senior students be interested in a design contest, conceptualizing a residential community of 600 acres with a golf course in the center?"

"I'm sure a few would think about that. It sounds like something that could earn extra credit. You said it is a contest; is there a financial prize, or a simple plaque?"

"I represent a businessman who wants to remain anonymous. He suggested a five hundred dollar prize," Mike answered.

"That's a lot of work for a five hundred dollars. If you could double that, I'm pretty sure some of our brightest and best would enter. When do you need it?"

"He's not in any hurry; what would work best for the

student's time frame?" Mike was fishing again.

The professor said, "Give me a week to advertise it, and three weeks to complete it. By January 15th then?"

Mike said that was most doable, then gave the general description and dimensions of the property, and surrounding features of highway and river. He requested that the half acre lots along the river be situated with a wide view rather than a deep one from the road. Without knowing it, Venite Village was emerging with a life of its own.

Christmas was a spectacular festival at Blessed Sacrament. Both Christmas Eve services were at capacity, with the Vesper Singers leading singing and offering inspiration. A highlight for Fr. Mike was the conversation he had with his mom after the early service. She told him she was going to sell the house and find an apartment near the church so she could attend all the time. "You are the only part of my life that makes sense. I don't want to miss any more of it."

With a big hug, he thanked her for the best gift.

# Reality Bites

By the middle of January, three important events coincided. The White's had the Village site brush-free, with three large burn piles that had to dry out a bit before they could ignite them. Secondly the Architecture department had a clear design winner. There were two notable runners up that deserved notice. Mike generously gave them a five hundred dollar second place. And thirdly Ray Kellogg was invited to the Bishop's office to clear up his formal charges against Fr. O'Malley.

"Come in and be seated, Mr. Kellogg," the Bishop invited. "I would offer you a cup of tea but this is not a social call. You filed a formal complaint against Fr. O'Malley of the Blessed Sacrament Church and I'd like you to know the disposition of that action." Ray Kellogg had a confident smile. "This action has taken up more than a month of my office's time and effort. I'm not sure if this was an honest mistake on your part or a capricious misuse of my time and office." The smile was gone. "I have interviewed the staff and many members of Blessed Sacrament, and I have viewed hours of security footage. Fr. O'Malley is at the church seven days a week and averages 14 hours a day. He has taken no vacation in three years. The conclusion I have arrived at is that you are a dangerous little man, with a critical view of something that has been wonderfully refreshing to Blessed Sacrament. I also interviewed Fr. Michaels because you have so adamantly sung his virtue. It was a surprise to him, because you were a constant source of irritation and frustration to him. In fact, he believes he went into retirement two years earlier than planned due to your constant haranguing. You obviously didn't like him either."

Mr. Kellogg opened his mouth to argue with the Bishop, then decided to be still.

"I went to Salem to visit Miss Levine in the Corrections facility. You have called her vile names and accused her of immoral activity. Do you know what I found? A young woman who is putting her life together following a horrific family experience. The 'Love Letters,' you so eagerly slurred have been placed in a notebook for all the women to read. She had seventeen pages, one for each week she has been there, of positive encouragement and ideal advice. I asked her if there had been romantic notes from Fr. O'Malley, and she laughed at such a preposterous thought. She clearly told me there had been no other communication with him, and no personal visits from anyone other than me. I was interested to hear that after just one visit to Blessed Sacrament, she had been so impressed by the liturgy and the homily that she started the '51 Club.' Do you have any idea what that might be?" Mr. Kellogg shook his head. "It's a gathering of women before breakfast every morning to read the fifty-first Psalm, which was the homily text, that she insists has been life-changing. She is doing excellent work in her courses of study, and has been a model prisoner. Yet you decided to besmirch her with deeds that only exist in your mind. There is something dark and sinister in your complaint against Fr. O'Malley. I believe you need help, Mr. Kellogg, but it will not be at the expense of any other priest, or in any catholic church in the Portland area. I have asked Claire Moore the secretary at Blessed Sacrament to remove your name and your family members' from the membership role and I have urged all other churches to avoid your inclusion with them, until you have had psychiatric help. It is one thing for you to pledge generously to the finance campaign, and give such a pittance. Do you know that one year on your magnanimous $2500 pledge you paid just $10 dollars? That should be an embarrassment to you. Allowing you to rant and rage against decent and devout priests is an embarrassment I will not tolerate. Get some counseling, Mr. Kellogg; get some psychological help. You are an emotionally unstable man. For your family's sake, see a doctor." The Bishop was finished, save for a quick and heartfelt prayer: "O Compassionate Lord God, tonight we pray that you would save us from all that makes life useless and ugly, the hateful judgment that sees only twisted results. I pray for Ray, and his family. Save us from the unteachable spirit which will not learn; the ungrateful spirit that knows not how to say 'thanks;' the unhappy spirit which is filled with complaints and discontent. Let the healing of your grace begin today in this man, in Jesus name, and for his sake. Amen." He opened the door, signaling Mr. Kellogg to stand and leave. Tears were on both of their faces.

While that conference was concluding, Mike was in the Portland State Architect Department picking up three sets of designs. He was fully aware that what he was involved with was not Blessed Sacrament business. None-the-less, this was amazingly exciting. When he carried the rolls of paper into his study, Claire was beside herself to know what new plans were to be revealed. Mike tried to say that it was not about the church, but she didn't believe him. He was aware that the plans had to be placed elsewhere or prying eyes would be too curious to control.

It was late in the rectory, and he was pouring over the plans again. When seen in a perspective where each tiny square represented a quarter or half acre building lot, this babe was big! "I wonder if we could embellish this area by bringing in a water..." Breaking glass in the parlor made him start with a jolt. Mike ran for his batons. He was wearing gym shorts and a green army t-shirt. He slid into the parlor just as the door swung open. Ray Kellogg lurched in with an angry expression. Mike could hear Len coming down the stairs too.

"You have destroyed my life you .... monster!" Ray rambled. He still wore his white shirt and sport coat; but he was rumpled and disheveled. "You know you got me kicked out, and my family too. I hate you!"

"You are way out of control, Ray. Let's sit down and think this through."

The desperate man said, "You're not going to fool me again. I'm going to settle this tonight!" His hand came out of his jacket holding a pistol.

"Ray, you are a rational man, and what you are doing isn't. Please sit down." Mike took a couple short steps toward him and dropped one foot back as a brace.

"You have destroyed this church, and now I'm going..." His hand began to lift the muzzle of the gun toward Mike.

The half second rule still applied. The baton was just a blur as it struck the wrist above the gun. The sound of impact was sharp and harsh as bones shattered! The other baton shot forward like a spear, striking the exposed abdomen full force. There was the start of a scream that was cut off by a gasp and Mr. Kellogg collapsed in a heap. Without turning, Mike said, "Fr. Len, would you please call the police and ask them to bring an ambulance?" The entire episode had taken less than ten seconds from start to finish. The host of people who watched the security tape, which had recorded it all, were not sure if Mike could have done anything more to avoid it, but they were sure that Mr. Kellogg didn't have a chance once he took the crisis to its explosive tipping point. He was no match for a prepared Fr. O'Malley.

A gray stormy Sunday seemed to set the mood for the mass. Folks who hadn't heard about the trouble at the rectory were shocked by the news. "Fr. O'Malley actually struck him?" "He had a gun?" "Felony assault?" Those who had heard the news were saddened by the fact that the Kellogg's had been long-time members, and now Ray was in jail. "What will happen to Fr. O'Malley?" They all held their breath for the answer to that question.

The Bishop called on Tuesday, January 24th requesting Mike to attend a meeting that evening. When he arrived he found Fr. James, and Fr. Len there as well. When they were seated, the Bishop led them in prayer and then began: "Thank you again for this sudden meeting. It is a very unusual situation." He looked at Mike with a warm smile. "I feel so responsible for the incident. I was upset when I learned how abusive Mr. Kellogg had been to Fr. Michaels. No wonder that marvelous priest wanted out. He had been hounded from the very first day. I think I wanted Mr. Kellogg to know how totally unacceptable his behavior has been, and how marvelous yours has been at the same time. I loaded the gun he carried, so to speak. He just took it out on you."

"That being said," the Bishop took a deep breath, "there are some in the church who think you used excessive force. Both bones in his forearm were broken. They have recommended that I take some punitive action against you." The room was quiet, each man weighing the matter. "I do not want to do that for a number of reasons. First of which is I thought you were right in self defense. He was armed with a lethal weapon. But secondly, from a purely selfish reason, Lent begins in two weeks and Blessed Sacrament is the poster child for Catholicism in Portland. I don't want to do a thing to mar that. Lastly, I believe there is a negative image of the priests right now, and I hate to punish one who has been a model of virility, strength and honor." More silence filled the room.

Fr. Len spoke up: "I was in the room when Ray barged in. I wasn't sure what should happen until I saw the gun. Then I was grateful that Mike handled it the way he did. All of us could have been serious injured." More silent moments crept by.

Mike said, with a sigh, "I've never had much patience for other people's stupidity. It has always seemed like self-inflicted wounds. I am sorry for Ray's injury, but only if he doesn't learn something from it. I'd like to think that it might be the birth-pain of understanding for him, and a demonstration of practical limits of his behavior. I'm feeling extremely frustrated in the fact that the church wants strong leadership, as long as it is harmless; they seem to want dynamic direction as long as it is controllable by them."

Fr. James finally said, "Other's bad behavior must not be

a reason for us to punish the innocent. Mike, I think your action was merited and honorable. You tried to warn him; you gave him ample opportunity to avoid the consequences. You must not feel in any way criticized now. I also think it is a time of confusion that would benefit from a cooling off period. I'm thinking you should have a three month study sabbatical, all expenses paid, with luxury lodging on the fourth floor of the men's dorm; your old room is empty right now. You can choose to audit classes, or use it as a time of prayer. If you would like to use it for travel, or pleasure, do so. You deserve a vacation. And we should help make it a pleasant one."

The Bishop warmed to the idea, "That is such a good idea, Fr. Preston. I have a discretionary fund that will happily add five hundred dollars to the church's stipend, and of course you may use the church's Ford if you like." He was seeing that this was a suggestion of merit, allowing any critic satisfaction, and any proponent something to cheer about. "Mike, I hope you know that I consider you God's twentieth century Gideon, a marvelous man of valor. I hope you return to the pulpit on the first Sunday of May refreshed and affirmed by all." He prayed a blessing prayer, not knowing that it was the last time Mike would ever be in that room.

Back at the rectory, Mike packed his clothes in two large suitcases. He had a couple boxes of books and papers. His batons rested on top of the pile. When Fr. Len came in he looked at the packing and said, "You are coming back?" When Mike assured him that it was only for three months, Len said, "Please promise me that is true. I have grown so comfortable expecting marvelous things each Sunday from you. Promise me!"

"You know I only get to use the car until the first of May.

I'll be back." But he didn't promise.

He called John White instead. "Hi Sergeant, can I buy you breakfast in the morning?" "Yeah, I thought maybe we could meet at 8:00 at the International House of Pancakes in Burlington; isn't that near your apartment?" "No, I'm on vacation." "Yeah, really, and I have something to show you that will make you salivate like a hound at a barbeque." "No, just you, if that's O.K." "Yup, I hear you." Mike could feel the excitement, which was always nearby, warming and becoming demanding. This was about to go crazy!

They were just finishing their pancakes when the server asked, "Looks like you've got a lot of paperwork there." She could see the long rolls of concept drawings. "Would you like to go into the banquet room? There are big tables and no one is in there." She may have been thinking about the family waiting for a table.

When John saw the drawing he sucked in some air, "Wow! That is huge! And do you think there will be a golf course in the middle? Is that what this is, a club house? Wow!"

"The first rough drawing I saw," Mike said, "had a multi use building that could be a restaurant, and on Sunday mornings a church. I think that's why it has such a big parking lot. And this area was designated as a clinic and a day care school.."

"Wow! It is hard to grasp."

"As I was driving here, this morning I thought of all the suggestions I could make to him about the development, but I know zip about it, so I thought you might have some experience."

"Nothing this big. But I do know it has to start with the county giving a permit to develop. Then utilities have to be approved and lined up. I'll bet it would be easier to get approval for a golf course, which is almost a park, which is public, than it would to get approval of a residential area that is more private. How many home sites are there here?"

"I don't know, there must be four or five hundred. But I think he has in mind just going to six or eight stages, instead of all at once. I'd sure like to have one of those riverfront ones."

John leveled a look at Mike and asked, "So are you just showing off, or is there a purpose to this morning?"

"I am so glad you asked," Mike said happily. "He really liked the way you guys scraped the brush off and wonders if you want a job. How would you like to be early construction manager for this project? At first it probably wouldn't be full time, but it might become that. You'd have to get to know the folks at the county courthouse. Do you think it would take more than three months to get the permits?

"Like I said, if it's a golf course, where some houses could be added I think, yeah, it could."

"Let's try it then. He is willing to offer you $1500 dollars a month for three months. It's a trial basis. If that works you may be in charge of the next phase, which would be getting the roads and utilities in. After that the fun really begins."

"Could I do some other jobs along with it if I have time?"

"Like I said, it would probably be part time at first, it's up to you. He just wants the work to begin."

"Then of course I want the job. If nothing else, it will get pa and me through this winter. By the way, when does it snow around here?"

"Let's go get some copies of this plan, and I have the property description from the Title company. When you need money for the permits, just let me know. I can usually get it from him in one business day."

"I hope you're getting something out of this. When I think about how big this is going to be, I know someone is going to make a fortune. By the way, I like you in civvies; that black get-up made you look like a funeral director."

On the way back to the school, Mike stopped at the Oregonian, where at the sport's desk, he was given the contact information for Ben Hogan. It took him almost an hour to compose a letter that sounded friendly and still business like. "Mr. Hogan. Thank you for considering this request. We are a non-profit group who are trying to design a new golf course near Portland Oregon. In our exuberance we thought of asking you to give us a concept drawing of an ideal course, the sort of place you would like to play. We have over 300 acres to put it in so there will even be enough room for duffers like me. We are not asking for topographical exactness, just the outline of the sort of place you would like to see. If you favor us with this, we will gladly make a thousand dollar donation to the charity of your choice. I will be glad to hear from you soon.

Yours cordially, Fr. Mike O'Malley" He used his school box as a return address.

While he was at it he sent a note to Leanne: "Learn to love challenge, and you will fill your life with accomplishment. Learn to love effort, and your skills will grow more valuable with each passing day. Learn to love making a difference, and doors will quickly open for you wherever you go. Learn to love giving freely of yourself, and you'll receive more fulfillment than you ever could imagine. Learn to love being the authentic person you are, and everything you do will be infused with integrity. Learn to love whatever work you are doing, and that work will bring abundant rewards. Learn to love beauty for beauty's sake, and you'll discover a wealth of it in places no one else would even think to look. Learn to love unconditionally, and there will be no limit to what your love can accomplish. Learn to love life just because it is, and each day will be a grand new adventure. Learn to love the moment you are in, and you will find richness in every direction. Learn to love the possibilities, and you will make your way to whatever you seek. Learn to love no matter what, and you will discover what a miracle you truly are. Good night Blessings, Fr. Mike

(Please note the address for the next three months.)"

The phone in the hall rang, and when he answered it the switchboard told him there was a call for him. "Hello this is Fr. O'Malley."

"Mike, its John. Are you busy?"

"Nope, just thinking about supper pretty soon."

"Then I'm glad I caught you. May I join you, or do you have a date."

"Listen, Hot Shot, there are lots of girls who would be happy to share my table."

"Yeah, if you paid for their dinner. I have got some really fun stuff I want to tell you about. Do I just show my muscle at the gate?"

"Just tell them you are my guest and they will point out the cafeteria. When will you be here?"

"Well, I'm about two blocks away, so when will you be there?"

"O.K. It's a race. Winner gets to buy. What am I saying; the Bishop gets to buy. I'll tell you about it." They both hung up and hurried as fast as they reasonably could.

"Hi Bertie," Mike greeted the woman behind the counter. "Yeah, I'm back for a study brush-up. Actually I missed your Rueben sandwiches. We'll each have one with fries."

As soon as they found a table in the corner away from the crowd, John said, "I've been a busy boy today. I've got a lot to tell you, and ask. But the first question is, what's this B.S. about an eccentric investor? I figured it out the first day. There is no 'He,' is there. Is it just you and me doing this thing? Do you have anyone else on it?"

Mike looked into John's eyes, seeing a brother and not an adversary. "I have been sitting on this secret for four years, not knowing what the heck to do with it. I'll share it with you because I have come to see you as my brother. You're right; it is just you and me. The purchase of the land was a fleece to see if it might happen. I feel like I am just walking behind a chain of events."

"But Mike, whose money is it, and how much do you have?"

"It may have been some crook's thirty or forty years ago. Somebody killed him for it, then someone else stole it from him; someone else hid it, and then died. There is no way to tell who had it last. The guy who asked me to get it for him, died the very next day. Nobody but you, and my friendly attorney know about it."

John asked, "How much is there, thousands?"

Mike paused, hesitant to let out the truth. "Would you believe four and a half million?"

"God damn! 'Scuse me father. That's enough to just live a life of ease," John said quietly.

"It would be. But then we would miss the greatest

adventure of our lives."

"What's your big plan for this thing then," John asked.

"John, I don't have a plan," Mike said sincerely. "This thing has a life of its own. I didn't know you and your dad would be available. I just go with what's in front of me. So far it has been super. Yesterday I sent a letter to Ben Hogan for a golf course design. I'll bet he does it. Just whatever is in front of me; I take the target."

John responded with fresh enthusiasm, "Let me tell you what I learned yesterday. I talked to the County exec, who said a golf course would be a high priority for the area, just like we thought. He said we would need to have the land surveyed, to mark off the streets. I didn't know what sort of a name might go on the project, so I said it was going to be a veteran's memorial. He loved it, and said he would personally walk it through the hoops. He gave me a contact at Puget Power and Energy for electricity; and the contact for sewers. He also told me about a new business that is just getting started. Summit Construction does a systems built home on their site, in two or three parts that can be moved and assembled on sight in less than half the time of a stick built home that Pa and I could put together, and at less cost. You can't tell the difference. I guessed the next step was up to the survey folks, so I asked about their availability. They can start within the week, but it will cost forty grand." His face was concerned.

"If that's the target that's in front of us, let's take the shot", Mike said with confidence. "Do you want to tell them or should I?"

"Which one of us is getting paid, right now?" John had a twinkle in his eye. "I've never been part of anything this big, or fun. It's like a fantasy."

"In my imagination," Mike said, "I see you and your dad building nice homes for a long time. It will be crucial to get these lots sold. It's like a game of pick-up sticks. We just need to be careful with each step."

John was still for a moment, then said, "I'm wondering if there is something Judy can help with; maybe she could be our bookkeeper. That would make the money go further too."

"Shall we agree to have supper again tomorrow evening?" Mike asked, changing the subject. "And I would also appreciate keeping this private right now, just between the two of us. We have a little advantage until everyone knows about it. Then there could be more trouble than we want." John wasn't sure what he meant, but could tell that it was a word of caution.

By the end of February there were flags marking the road and building sites of the development, and a grader was putting contours into Mr. Hogan's sketch, even adding a narrow lake with water from the river through a culvert under the road. He had thanked Mike for the donation to Danny Thomas' St. Jude Hospital. He also agreed to visit the third weekend of May, 1962 for an invitational tournament on the new golf course. Portland Paving was the low bid for placing a blacktop road, and sweetened the plan by offering to do the main parking lot at the same time for half price. Fr. Len had made four lunchtime visits to chat; Mike knew it was time to tell the Bishop.

# Resignation and Realization

"Good morning Bishop Morris," he wrote. "This sabbatical has been the perfect time to reconsider my recent actions, and future plans. I want you to know how grateful I am for the opportunity to have a place in Christ's Church. Your guidance and assistance has been wonderful. In an ideal world a pacifist army would be in complete accord with God's Word. My experience, however, is that we still need police and armed warriors to maintain justice and order, and a safe community. This time of prayer has led me to see that while I'm a pretty good 90% fit for the priesthood, I am not completely in keeping with standards and expectation for continued service, and I am not willing to disarm myself. That militant 10% of me will be a perpetual irritation or aggravation to whatever congregation I may be serving. Therefore please accept my resignation from the priesthood, effective May 1st 1961. The memories of four years of service will be lasting treasures. May God bless your clear and faithful leadership. Mike O'Malley."

Copies were sent the Frs. James, Len and Kent.

He also wrote to Leanne, but didn't mention the resignation. "Good morning. I hope it is a sparkling new day for you. Here's a helpful thought , 'Sometimes, when things fail to go the way you planned, they actually turn out better than you could have possibly expected. Welcome life's surprises and choose to see the positive value that is in each one of them. Don't be too quick to place judgments on the people, situations, and events in your life. In everything that comes along, there is an opportunity for you to more fully discover and express your true purpose.'"

"This study time has been an eye-opener for me. Writing these positive thoughts to you has reminded me that the most reliable path to success is a simple one that anyone who chooses to do so can follow. Dream big dreams, and take small steps, one after another after another, until you are there. Whether something is possible or impossible for you depends more on your attitude than anything else. Your persistent, focused action is what brings possibilities to life. Blessings, Fr. Mike."

March was given to negotiating the next steps. John talked to the folks at Cascade Nursery for two thousand trees. He also got bids from three landscapers for the clubhouse and waterfeature. Finally with a permit, Mike pressed the utilities to begin down the north side of the property. He also went back to the School of Architecture with another design contest, this time for the multi-purpose club house. It had to be large enough for a pro shop, restrooms, and a café. His final challenge was getting Summit Construction to see the scope of his idea. They could make an affordable three bedroom, two bath house within two months, from selection of interior finishes to installation. They were dubious about his claim that there would be orders for six a month for the next three or four years! Finally Mike offered to pay cash for three of their top designs, to be installed as model homes by July. One of them had to have an additional room in the front to become a sales office. Summit Construction got the picture, and the order to begin immediately.

April was a particularly quiet month. John and his dad went back to Oklahoma so a wedding could take place. Without his companionship, Mike had little reason to visit the project site daily. There was the planting of an English Hawthorn hedge along the highway side of the property, but that was of little interest after about an hour. He returned to school and wrote another note to Leanne.

To his delight, there were two Department of Correction envelopes in his mailbox. The first one was a happy announcement from Leanne that she had finished her first wave of studies in Bookkeeping with honors. She had also finished her GED high school equivalence, again with flying colors. She thanked him for his encouragement and his confidence in her. It wasn't easy, but following his lead, it was an accomplishment that gave her much pride.

The second one, that must have been written later, was a tender admission that while she had many sweet friends around her, there was no one who could hold her in strong arms. She admitted that his was the only face she could imagine in this quiet time. She apologized if this was an inappropriate conversation, but he had told her to write, and he would answer. "So, I'm writing to tell you that just the touch of your hand was so warm and sweet, it has kept a little fire warming my heart. I know I am just a lonely girl, so I don't expect a gushy response. I just want you to know that you have found a tender spot in my heart, and I'm grateful. Thanks for listening. Leanne"

Mike reread the letter twice, feeling a lot like a teenager at the thought of a girl liking him. He answered her with a note of appreciation, sharing that he too remembered the warmth of her hand and the smell of her hair. He was not comfortable remembering more.

April ended with Mike finding a furnished apartment in Burlington that he could call home. He returned the Ford to Blessed Sacrament, and bought a used Buick station-wagon from Olsen Buick from the accumulated disability checks that had been placed in his savings account. He was on his own.

John and Judy returned in May, just in time to see the white sugar sand dumped in the many sand traps. One final dressing of the fairways and greens allowed the seeding. Then the golf course just had to sprout and grow. On the other hand, the Club house/Cafe plan came from the architects with a sensational design. John looked at the sweeping glue-lam beams and glass front. This truly would be the centerpiece of the entire project.

"You know," he said with his typical grin, "Pa and I could probably build this if we hired three or four good workers to help us."

"What sort of bid would you think appropriate?" Mike didn't mean that to sound more business-like than friendly.

"It would depend on these beams, but I'm thinking in the range of ninety five to a hundred thousand. It truly is a simple construction with poured concrete side walls and steel supports. The entire roof is two by six tongue and groove lumber, with a foam and plywood covering, and concrete shakes. It's like a grown-up's tinker toy. But I don't think it should be on a slab, but a utility basement graded out and the same sort of lumber floor. It would make it much more handy to have all the furnace, heat ducts, plumbing and wiring down there and warm attractive wood up here. That might be just a touch more money, but it will make it up in convenience and safety."

Mike thought for a moment, then said brightly, "All our bills are paid and we still have about a third of the 'investor's' money. There are still a lot of little things, but this is the last major piece for the beginning phase. Let's take the shot! I'll count on you and Jerry. Precisely twelve months from now we will have a world class golf tournament. I think it will all be ready."

There were two notes from Leanne in his mailbox. He treated them like something fragile. "Hello. I hope you are alright, with a new address, again. And you didn't sign it Fr. Mike. Are you in trouble with the Bishop? I hope not."

"I thought we would take the summer off from school, but that is only for kids, I guess. I get to learn to type and a second class is just called office management. I think it will be very interesting."

"I'm afraid I don't know how to be shy or coy. I have an invitation that's pretty big. Do you think you could drive down to Salem and visit me? I've been here eight months and my only visitor has been the Bishop. That's why I thought you might be in trouble. Visiting hours are Saturday from 3 to 5. It would be so grand to see you again. I'm praying that you will say, 'yes'! Your lonesome friend, Leanne"

The second one was a clincher for Mike; she quoted him back to himself, "Hello friend, I suppose you haven't even had time to answer the last letter, and here comes another. Are you getting the idea that I really like you? I do! I really do!"

"You once wrote, 'Many of life's best rewards are possible only because you must work your way through difficult challenges to get to them. If everything in life were easy, there would be no opportunity for real fulfillment. Life is not always easy; and because of that, you have the opportunity to make it truly great.'"

"That is absolutely true! It is not easy in here, but you told me how to work my way through the difficulties and I have found real fulfillment for the first time in my life. My counselor has given me some very hopeful news. Because of my good attitude and hard work, she believes my time has been reduced. I hope I get the chance to tell you what a champion you are to me. Thank you. Your hopeful friend Leanne. P.S. 3 to 5!"

For the rest of the week, Mike had an on-going conversation with himself, arguing why that would be a silly idea, unwise, risky, and inexcusably irrational. But he couldn't put the idea aside, so at noon Saturday he headed south on highway 99 for Salem.

They sat in a white room, at a white table, her in white coveralls with OCI letters on the back. It was pretty colorless. But for the two of them it was a field of spring blossoms and they were by themselves instead of surrounded by a dozen other tables with visitors. He had explained that the sergeant from Korea was in charge of the golf course project and there was plenty of work to do right now. He told her about the wedding in Oklahoma and the new bride. Yes, they were a cute couple and would probably have darling kids. He wasn't sure why he felt like holding her hand, but when he reached toward her hand, she quickly reached for his too. Mike said he forgot what they were talking about and her laughter was like pleasant music. Finally, he explained about Mr. Kellogg and the night stick trouble.

"You said he had a gun?" she asked. "How is that not self-defense?"

"Well, it was, and it was caught on the security cameras so there was no doubt that I tried to avoid it. But there were folks in the church that thought I hit him a little too hard. I wonder how hard they would have popped him if it had been them he was about to shoot." Mike's smile was relaxed and gentle.

"Are you going to miss all your priest duties?" He loved the way she wrinkled her nose.

"Some, and I'll miss the staff I had. But in my letter of resignation, I told the Bishop I was only 90% priest. The other 10% was too precious to me to ignore." There was that deep level look with brown eyes. It was like she was peering within him.

She whispered with a grin, "I really liked the 90% I got to see. I hope you know that I am giving you credit for opening my life to a higher more constructive Leanne. I also hope you know that I would welcome meeting that other 10%." She giggled like a girl.

The buzzer announced the end of the first hour visits. He had to go. She rose from her chair, and Mike was aware again how petite she was, standing on tiptoes to hug him. He still had to bend way over to kiss the side of her head. Like a sprite she seemed weightless and happy.

"Will you visit again next week, please, please," she begged. "There is so much I want to know about you, and tell you about myself," her voice was pleading.

"Maybe the following week. I'll see. We have three new homes moving in soon. They are the model homes. Then I hope there will be lots of interest in construction. That's my job." It wasn't an outright rejection, and to Leanne there was a possibility, which a girl could go on for another week.

He visited twice again in June; three times in July and every Saturday in August, even though the new mowers were delivered and the fresh groomed course took on a very finished appearance. He continued to write her daily messages of encouragement and positive reinforcement. John teased him saying that someone was acting like a guy in love. Mike remembered that this delightful lady, who seemed to be fresh and innocent, had made a career as a con artist. So there was still a part of the rational man who was on alert. But there was that other irrational part that was eager each week to hold her hand, hear her voice, or smell her hair.

The exterior of the clubhouse was finished by mid September and it was glorious. John wondered what should be done with the large amount of dirt that had been removed for the basement. His dad suggested that they build an elevated first tee box with it, and use the side toward the parking lot to make a stone water-feature and a sign with the course name. John said it would be a great place for a huge American flag.

He called Mike early the first Monday in October, saying, "You better get over here; we've got trouble." Mike hurriedly dressed and drove over to find four of the big front windows shattered. A note under a rock said, "Window insurance is four hundred a month, or this will happen again and again."

Mike called the police with a complaint, and pretty quickly a patrol car swung into the parking lot. The concerned officer took pictures and statements. Mike assured him he had no idea who would try such a thing. But just to be sure, he called Leanne, using her counselor's number. When he heard her familiar voice he told her of the incident, and the shake down. She swore she knew nothing about it, but because her family was such a bunch of hooligans, she would make a couple calls. Yes, she thought this was absolute foolishness too. Would he call her soon? "Promise?" "Yes, I am hoping for that too." Her voice was tender and low. Then she asked Mrs. Stanley, her counselor, if she could make a call to Portland.

"Hello Uncle Caesar, it's Leanne. Yes, I'm still in prison" "Yes." "Hey, listen to me! Someone broke windows at the new golf course. Did you have anything to do with that?" "Come on, listen to me! Did - you – have - anything to do with that?" "Oh, you know someone who might know about it, huh?" "Quit trying to change the subject. The guy who is working out there is my special friend. He is the only one who has visited me here, that's why I want to know." "Yeah, I'm thinking he might be the future father of my kids. So that's what!" "Listen to me, you wop bastard, I said did you do it?" "O.K. fine, you say you might have done it. So here's what I want you to do, go fix the damned windows. I don't care how much they cost. You broke them, now you fix them today, you got that?" "You old fart, stop hedging on me. You will do it today or I will tell dad about you and mom." "Yes I would." "Of course I've known. I had to wash the stinky sheets that smelled like your cologne every time you visited." "He would still be mad enough to shoot your bony ass! Now get those windows fixed." "Yes, today! And make sure that nothing else is damaged. Do you understand me? Not one blade of grass, or I will punch your ticket." "Yeah, you too."

When she hung up, Leanne looked at Mrs. Stanley with a

shake of her head. "Some of the time family can be very trying, can't they?" She didn't know it, but she had just earned a parole recommendation from her counselor.

# Paroled to New Possibilities

Leanne called his apartment the Monday morning before Thanksgiving. "Oh Sweet Man, I was just told that I am paroled this afternoon. Isn't that fabulous?" When Mike agreed there just couldn't be any happier news, she asked if he could drive to Salem and pick her up.

"Just tell me what time to be there. I'll leave right away." As it turned out they had to wait until mid afternoon for all the paperwork to be done. When she stepped out the front door of the corrections building she pirouetted gracefully.

When she slid into the front seat beside Mike, she let her hand rest on his thigh as she proclaimed the joys of freedom. Again and again she laughingly noted the simple attractions they were passing; a church, a drive in restaurant, a beauty salon. All were fresh treats to her eyes. He was aware that her fingers were rhythmically stroking his thigh, moving ever so gently upward. Finally when he was afraid that an erection was beginning, he placed his hand over hers, stopping the stroking and the progressively intimate movement.

"Kiddo, you know how I feel about that. For me, sex goes with marriage. It's the most complete merger between us, and I can't, or won't, do that without pledging my whole life to you." He lifted her hand away.

"Mike, I feel that way too. I'm just more honest than you

are. I know that I have never given myself to a man, but I really want you. Can't we celebrate? I feel so happy, I have to do something wonderful." She started to place her hand on his thigh again, only to be intercepted and moved back to her own lap. They teased each other playfully all the way to Portland. She finally bluntly asked him to take her to his apartment so they could have some privacy, and Mike insisted on taking her to her own home where they wouldn't. He didn't see her again for five days.

On Saturday morning she knocked on his apartment door. When he opened it, he was shocked to see a fresh cut on her eyebrow, and a swollen bruise below her eye.

"My gosh, Leanne, what happened. Did your dad do that?"

"Yeah. You didn't warn me that French was paroled too. He must have something on a judge, because he certainly doesn't have good behavior."

Mike said defensively, "I had no way of knowing that. Can I get you a cold towel or an aspirin?" Her lovely face looked painful.

"Are we still drinking that good tea?" Then she told him that when she got home French was already there. Between him and her dad, they had four or five marks lined up to start that old shake-down crap all over again. She had said definitely not; she had no intention of ever going back to prison. Last night, her dad had smacked her a couple times and then said that it was enough evidence to lay on any mark. Finally she had feigned vomiting, and retired to her room. This morning they were gone, but she was sure they would put the pressure on her again.

They enjoyed a pot of tea while Mike tried to think of

some way to get out of the perplexing paradox. She wasn't safe in her own home; and he wasn't safe with her in his. But his dilemma was a moral one, not a physical danger; and it was compounded by the realization that he had come to deeply love her, and desired all that was implied by those tender feelings. Finally he asked her if he could show her Venite Village and the Veterans Memorial Golf Course. She said she was very eager to see it.

As they drove in the wide driveway, she admired the attractive Venite Village sign. "It's so easy to see and read. I love the bright blue." Then when they made a loop in the parking lot so she could see the side and front of the Club house there were more exclamations. "Is this a café, or a church? It is so big and bold; this is beautiful!"

Mike took the loop road around the south side. "John and his dad are building these two places, and those two are from Summit Construction. It is weird to see the truck bring a portion of a house in, and three hours later it's on a foundation and they have the rest moving into place." They drove for a couple minutes around the west end, all empty lots. Then they came to eleven new Summit Construction homes all complete, and finally to the three model homes. "Would you like to see inside one?" It was fun to hear her happy approval of each room and the careful interior decorating.

"Mike, where is all this money coming from?" she asked incredulously. "This is fabulous, but I think real expensive."

"Yeah, I think he has deep pockets. It's a private investor who managed to get a lot of government surplus land. Now broken into individual lots, he'll make a wad of money."

"And are you getting paid on commission as you sell the

lots, or have you been on salary?" It was an honest question that had to have a dishonest answer.

"Mostly I have been paid by the individual job. He tells me to do something and then pays me for that." Mike shrugged.

"Well that doesn't sound very permanent to me. Will you have a future here?" She was more than a little interested, because since last Monday about all she could think about was how excited she was in his company and how aroused. She wanted to share his future. "Hey, is there a phone I could use? I'd like to call home."

"Yeah, there is one in the sales office. I wanted to show you that model too." Mike was a little on edge wondering what Leanne may need to share with her father, especially after talking about how expensive this place seemed. Actually, he heard her make two separate calls, speaking briefly and quietly both times.

"Hey, Kiddo," a name Mike was growing more fond of with every use, "It's kind of late for lunch and early for dinner, but I'm sort of hungry, how about you?" She said that she had missed breakfast, and thought the empty feeling in her stomach was just eagerness to see him.

Mike offered, "There is a steak house, or the Red Lion dining room."

She said with extra sparkle, "Let's go to the nearest one. I don't want to waste special time just riding in the car."

While they dined, chatted, laughed, and looked deeply into each other's eyes, they were also aware of the scrutiny from the server who was obviously critical of anyone who would bruise such a darling face. Thinking of those bruises, Mike was distracted by the thought that Leanne had given her dad an important message. Even as they drove back to his apartment the question nagged at him, but not enough to spoil their pleasant enjoyment of the other's closeness and warmth. She hooked her arm under his, pulling him tightly against her breast.

Once inside his apartment he guided her to the sofa. He sat down before she could, then gently tugged her to straddle his lap so they could be face to face. Their kiss was slow, and very passionate. Leanne was captivated by his intent, and determined to express her intent as well. She was happily unaware of the drama that was building into a crisis at the Levine Furniture warehouse.

Paul Levine and former police Lt. Sam French had been joined by the three security men Paul kept near him when trouble might be close. He had just said to French that he had heard there was a lot of money the former police officer was enjoying these days, like a fortune he had found. He pulled his .45 pistol to emphasize the importance of the topic. The three security men followed the motion. French slid his .38 revolver out of his shoulder holster, but did not brandish it openly.

Mike kissed her again, gently, but lingeringly; she had the fragrance of peaches. His hand stroked her hair and neck. She let her hand trail across his chest and reached behind him so she could press even tighter to him. Her hips rocked rhythmically on his lap.

Caesar entered the warehouse just then, noting the drawn weapons, so he, and the three security men he had, followed by drawing theirs as well. French was in the midst of a loud denial, claiming no knowledge of Paul's accusation. Voices were beginning to take a loud brittle edge. Each man was operating from a different agenda of information. French was thinking he was about to replace Caesar as the number two guy in Paul's organization. Leanne, however, had told her father that French had found the hidden cache of money that they had been searching for. In actuality, he had been spending the Loomis money, ripped off from the dead robbers. Caesar, regrettably, had been told by Leanne that Paul knew about the affair with her mom, and was going to get even. The boiling point was just about to spill over.

Mike unbuttoned Leanne's blouse and caressed the smooth softness within it. She moved more vigorously against his lap. Finally, he scooped her in his arms and carried her to the bedroom, where satisfaction awaited.

Caesar cut into French's denial by saying that he never intended to fall in love with Janice. The use of her name triggered the disaster. Slow motion examination of the security tape revealed that Paul shouted, "Liar!" Whether it was directed at French or Caesar was unclear. As he turned toward Caesar, he was shot in the chest twice by French. The half second rule was still in operation; Paul's pistol barked twice at Caesar, pointblank. Then it seemed that all nine pistols were firing at random; and men were falling in the same manner. When the last shell was fired, every one of them had taken at least one bullet. Seven men lay dead. French had at least five center mass wounds. He was dead before he hit the floor.

Mike removed her clothes as if unwrapping a priceless fragile treasure. He laid down, drawing her over him like a silk sheet. Only after her body had trembled in satisfaction for the third time, could Leanne say breathlessly, "Oh, I love you, for all my life! I've been told that the first time might be disappointing. That was wonderful."

Mike whispered into her warm neck, "I can't imagine loving you more," He kissed her smooth skin, then added, "But I can imagine loving you again!" He drew her to him amidst her giggles. "You have completely corrupted me, and I am very grateful."

Caesar's funeral was on Thursday, and Paul's was on Friday. Only a few mourners attended, mostly employees of their businesses who were unsure about their future. Both men were cremated so there was no graveside service.

# Concluding surprise

Mike and Leanne sat in the luxury home on the west hill Leanne had inherited. Mike had helped empty the closets and drawers of her dad's clothes and personal junk. They had found a variety of guns, and several caches of money. Finally it had been sanitized of the horde of bad memories she wanted behind her. They were leafing through the family picture album, finding memories she wanted to keep. Leanne explained how it had come about that she was the only Levine left. "This is Aunt Bernie, she was mom's sister, who got a fever when they were in Mexico. She might have made it if she could've seen a doctor." "Yeah, that's Patsy, Uncle Caesar's' first wife." "Yeah, she's cute. She was lost in a poker game, and went away with the winner." "This one is Grandpa Levine, Jacob I think. He was a bootlegger." "Yeah but he was shot by the competition." "That's my folks when they first moved to Portland." "I know; she could have been a model. Dad never got over her loss." "I think it was a venereal disease, but he always just called it an infection." "That's Dot, Uncle Caesar's second wife; she took her own life with an overdose. The story I heard was that she had VD too." "Yeah real sad. That's sort of the story of my family. It's just me now, with no living relative." Hugging him to her she said, "It's just us now." "Oh, that was my half brother Marco; I think he died in the Philippines, or

else he went AWOL and moved in with some hot local lady. The Army classified him as dead when I was just a little girl."
"No, that's my maternal grandmother, Granny Carrel. They were not real happy with our side of the family. I think they were farmers in North Dakota. It was a hard life that took them pretty young. I think I only saw her twice."

Mike asked, "Wait. Did you say her name was Carrel? Did she by any chance have a grandson named Ernie?"

"Yeah, he was my cousin. His dad died in the war in think, and his mom passed away from cancer in the nursing home a few years ago. He lived with us for a while, but he died in prison about five years ago. Did you know him?"

"Oh Sweetheart, I have such a long story to tell you, about your complicated inheritance."

She rubbed her breast against his arm. "Well, I love bedtime stories, and I have a lifetime to listen." She kissed him in a way that suggested that the rest of the story might need to wait a while to be told.